Sleeping Sands

A Magical Mystery

MARION SHAW

authorHOUSE®

AuthorHouse™ UK
1663 Liberty Drive
Bloomington, IN 47403 USA
www.authorhouse.co.uk
Phone: 0800.197.4150

Published by AuthorHouse   05/15/2015

ISBN: 978-1-5049-4264-5 (sc)
ISBN: 978-1-5049-4263-8 (e)

Print information available on the last page.

This book is printed on acid-free paper.

CONTENTS

CHAPTER 1 – RAINBOWS

Chloe ran up the steps as fast as she could, trying to reach the safety of the trees at the top of the garden. She looked over her shoulder to see a huge shape behind her and it was gaining on her!

She slipped on the last step and fell face-first into the grass at the top of the steps. She rolled over, there was an animal was standing over her and it was so big it was blocking out the sun throwing her into shadow. Before she could move her arms to protect her face, a big wet tongue licked her from her chin right up to her forehead. She tucked stray strands of hair away behind her ear and laughed. Her dog Raggie flopped down beside her, he was panting and had his tongue stuck out, he had a big doggie grin on his face as he rested in the shade of the tree. Raggie was a golden retriever and by far the friendliest dog Chloe knew.

Chloe was lying on her back and she was half asleep when she heard a strange noise. "Psst, over here!" Chloe sat up and looked around trying to find out where the sound was coming from, but she couldn't see anything. Raggie had walked over to the Cherry Blossom tree and was wagging his tail. Chloe stood up and followed Raggie but she couldn't see anything. She heard the noise again - it was right in front of her. She looked carefully at the tree and saw the strangest man standing in the grass beside the tree.

"Hello Chloe, my name is Peter I am a pixie and we really need your help" said the strange man in a friendly voice. Chloe couldn't help but stare; she had never seen a pixie before. She knew it was rude to stare but this was the strangest creature she had ever met. He had pointy ears and the greenest eyes she had ever seen. He was wearing green trousers, a brown shirt and a green hat with a leaf on it. His clothes seemed to change colour as he moved, which helped him blend into his surroundings so he was very difficult to see if you weren't concentrating hard.

"How do you know my name?" asked Chloe. "It was the Flower Fairies" Peter explained "They spend a lot of time in your garden, they like using your bird bath to cool down when it is very hot. They talk to Raggie all the time." Chloe looked a Raggie who was wagging his tail from side to side and nodding his head in agreement.

Peter looked around to see if there was anyone else nearby and whispered: "Please help us - the Sandman has disappeared! Humans are not getting enough sleep because the Sandman is not using his magic Sleeping Sand. If humans don't get enough sleep they don't have happy dreams. Happy dreams are full of magic and keep Fairyland alive and well. We need humans to have happy dreams to keep the magic alive in Fairyland. Tired humans are mean and grumpy and sometimes make children cry. Fairies are born when children laugh for the first time. Fairyland needs happy children and dreams to keep the magic alive and to create new Fairies for each new baby born in the human world. Every person has their own fairy. If we run out of magic we won't be able to create new Fairies and we won't be able to work our magic or fly any more". Peter was so upset he started crying.

"How can I help?" asked Chloe "I don't even know where Fairyland is!"

Raggie barked and nudged Chloe with his nose. Chloe looked at Raggie and said "Sorry Raggie I don't understand you".

"I can help" said Peter, he waved his hands at Raggie and said a few strange words. "Woof! Help Peter, we have to find the Sandman. I will come with you to help and protect you. You are very clever. I am sure that we can help Peter find the Sandman". Chloe looked around to see if there was another pixie she hadn't noticed.

"Woof, pay attention Chloe, Peter cast a magic spell so you can understand me" barked Raggie. Chloe looked curiously at Raggie and poked him in the side

"Woof - stop poking" barked Raggie. Chloe threw her arms about Raggie in a big hug.

"We are wasting time" said Peter "Are you coming?"
"Coming where?" asked Chloe. We need to go to Fairyland" said Peter "It is the only way to find the

3

Sandman". "Can we really go to Fairyland?" asked Chloe in excitement. "If you agree to help us, we will go there straight away" said Peter.

"We are next to one of the biggest stations in Fairyland". Chloe looked around and wondered how they would find this station, she was sure she would have noticed a station in her garden.

Peter turned around and went to the side of the Cherry Tree. He took a blue shiny rock from his pocket. He used the stone to draw the shape of a door on the trunk of the tree. To Chloe's amazement a door appeared in the trunk of the tree, there was a sign on the door. Chloe read the sign out loud: 'Blue entrance to Cherry Tree Station'.

Chloe stared at the door in amazement. "I have never seen that before, has it always been there? Where does it go?" she asked curiously. Peter explained that Fairyland could be reached from the human world by secret doors which could only be seen and opened by magic keys. Peter's key was in the shape of a stone.

Each of the main stations had seven entrances.

"They are red, orange, yellow, green, blue, indigo and violet" he said.

"Those are the colours of the rainbow" said Chloe. "Exactly! Wow - you are very clever" said Peter

"We use rainbows to connect everyone in Fairyland. When you see a rainbow the people of Fairyland are using it to travel from place to place."

"That door is very small" said Chloe doubtfully, "I don't want to get stuck, imagine being half in and half out of a tree!" "Don't worry" said Peter kindly "Fairy magic will take care of everything".

The door opened. Chloe, Raggie and Peter stepped into the tree. Inside they saw an amazing sight: the inside of the tree was much bigger than the outside. The roots of the tree curved around and created the walls of the station. The roots glowed brightly and lit up the room. The floor was brightly coloured and had different coloured paths leading away from the centre of the room to tunnels which wound around the roots of the tree and out of sight. They were standing on the blue path, it curved around a root and continued to the centre of the room. In the middle of the room there was a spiral staircase and around the outside of it was a slide. Above the staircase there was an arrow pointing down that said: 'Departures'.

"Come on, this way we must lead down to departures" said Peter cheerfully.

He went to the top of the slide and picked up a cushion, he put the cushion on the edge of the slide and sat down, then he slid down with a whoosh. Raggie disappeared down the slide on a blue cushion with paw prints on it. Chloe picked up a brightly coloured cushion from the pile and slid down the slide with a whoosh to the next level. Chloe was laughing in delight and wanted to run back up to the entrance level to do it all over again. As she picked herself up from the ground and immediately a little squirrel grabbed her cushion and scampered up a rope to the level above.

5

Chloe looked around for another cushion and stopped and stared in astonishment. This level was even more amazing than the one where they had entered the station. All around the edge of this level were tunnels and each tunnel had a name above it. They were the strangest names: 'Sandy beach', 'Windy Harbour', 'Sugarloaf Mountain', 'Bog of Frogs', 'Tide Pool Ridge', 'Craggy Nook', 'Little Fish Ponds' and many more.

"This is one of the seven main stations in Fairyland" explained Peter "This station links up with the other main stations as well the smaller stations in this region".

"The colours of the tunnels are different, why is that?" asked Chloe. Peter explained that the tunnels are colour-coded and relate to different regions of Fairyland. The rainbow coloured tunnels go to one of the other main stations. The red tunnels lead to the mountains, orange lead to the sandy desert, yellow to central Fairyland, green to the swamplands, blue lead to the coastland, indigo to the water region where all the lakes are and violet to the midlands. "Woof, I would like to see the sea ....I like swimming" barked Raggie. "We don't have time" said Peter "Come on, our tunnel is over there".

They walked towards one of the rainbow tunnels, the sign above the tunnel read 'Fairyland Central Station'. When they reached the tunnel there was a ramp leading to a platform. Beside the platform were several objects that looked train carriages as they had lots of seats and windows, but no wheels and no engine. These carriages were sitting on a rainbow -coloured road which stretched into a tunnel and disappeared off into the distance.

There was a conductor on the platform and he shouted: "Next departure in 5 minutes, take your seats please".

Raggie, Chloe and Peter hopped into an empty compartment.

"There are no wheels" said Chloe, "how do we get around?"

"Wait and see" smiled Peter.

"Last call........... All aboard" shouted the conductor.

When the last two Brownies were safely seated the conductor shouted

"Hold on please, off we go!"

The carriages lurched forward and slid along the rainbow at breakneck speed leaving a trail of rainbows behind them. Chloe laughed as she was having so much fun – she loved rollercoasters. Raggie had a doggy grin on his face and he had his tongue sticking out. Peter was quietly smiling at the enjoyment Chloe and Raggie were having. The other passengers were chatting and smiling at Chloe and Raggie. All too soon the ride was over. Chloe and Raggie looked sad that the carriage had stopped.

"Don't worry" said Peter "You'll have plenty of chances to ride the rainbow roads later".

They stepped out onto the platform. This station was like the Cherry Tree Station but was much bigger – at least ten times the size and had many more people and creatures milling around. There were goblins, fairies, elves, pixies and a few giants as well! In the centre of the room there was a spiral staircase and around the outside of it was a slide. Above the staircase there was an arrow pointing down and it said: 'Departures'. There was also a spiral staircase made from crystal going upwards. The sign said 'Level 3, Restricted Access'.

There was a big entrance across the station and above the opening there was a sign 'Reception, Shopping & Exit to Seree'. "What does Seree mean?" asked Chloe curiously. v"It means Peace and it is the name of our city" answered Peter "Come on he said we have no time to lose: follow me". Peter led Chloe and Raggie to the stairway which wound up towards level 3.

At the bottom of the stairway were four fearsome guards, each guard had a huge sword and they looked scary!

"Name and Purpose?" demanded one of the guards.

"Hello Iolo, how are you today? I have Chloe and Raggie here to see King Blackthorn and Queen Rose" said Peter. "Authorisation please?" said Iolo.

Peter took a shiny gold gem from his pocket. Iolo took a black stone from his sword and touched the two together. The gem glowed brightly with golden light and the sound of a pure bell was heard to echo across the station. "Authorisation granted, up you go" said Iolo.

Peter led the way up the staircase. Each step made a different sound, the notes echoed across the station. As they walked up the stairs each step lit up in one of the colours of the rainbow, Chloe was sure that it would be impossible to sneak up these stairs. They climbed high above the station through an opening in the roof onto level 3. At the top of the stairs was a beautiful crystal dome, from here Chloe and Raggie could see the Palace in the distance and the beautiful city around them. The station appeared to be in the centre of the city and the palace was towards the North of the city, in the distance huge mountains towered above the palace.

There was a crystal slide in this room which glowed softly as they approached.

"We don't need carriages here" Peter said.

"When we sit on the slide here, Iolo will activate the magic which will take us to the palace. This ensures that even if someone managed to get in here they couldn't go anywhere as an alarm would be triggered immediately and they would be captured". They picked up a pillow and sat on the crystal slide. A few seconds later the slide burst into light and they were sliding along, they could see the blur of Seree as they whooshed past. They landed in a crystal dome which was similar to the one in the station. All around the walls there were beautiful tapestries of animals, nature scenes and Fairy folk. Beside each tapestry they saw guards standing at attention.

The guards looked fearsome and Peter explained that they were the first line of defence in this part of the palace and they were some of the best warriors in all of Fairyland – there were two Fairies, one Giant, three Elves, one Pixie, one Leprechaun and two Dwarfs.

CHAPTER 2 – THE NOTE

Chloe and Raggie were very nervous as all the guards had weapons; some had swords, others axes and others bows. But strangely enough neither the Pixie nor the Leprechaun were visibly armed. Just as Chloe was about to ask Peter why they had no weapons, a segment of the wall disappeared and behind it stood two of the most beautiful Fairies Chloe had ever seen. Peter bowed and said "King Blackthorn, Queen Rose may I present Chloe and Raggie from the human world. They have kindly agreed to help us find the Sandman".

The King and Queen were graceful and they glowed with a soft light that radiated power. "Hello and welcome Chloe, thank you so much for agreeing to help us" said Queen Rose. King Blackthorn spoke directly to Raggie in a series of barks, and Raggie barked "Woof, I will". Chloe wondered what they had discussed but she had no time to find out as the King and Queen were gesturing to Chloe, Raggie and Peter to follow them.

They followed the King and Queen to their private chambers where they met the twins, Princess Daisy and Prince Ethan for the first time. They appeared to be slightly older than Chloe although Fairies age differently to humans so it was difficult to tell. The King and Queen explained that they believed that an evil Fairy was behind the plot to destroy Fairyland. So far they had been unable to find the Sandman and hoped that Chloe would be able to help them solve the clues and show them where the Sandman was so they could rescue him. Before the Sandman disappeared they had received a letter from a creature that referred to themselves only as Nyx. They showed the letter to Chloe.

To King Blackthorn and Queen Rose

We believe that Fairyland has become weak and is losing its power.

We no longer control human minds and have no influence over them. Traditionally we have used humans to complete tasks for us and have bewitched them when we wanted and when we needed to. This practice has been stopped under your rule and we believe it is making the Fairy race weak.

We are not in agreement with your policy of letting all creatures live peacefully in Fairyland and would banish the following races to the wild: Sprites, Elves, Pixies, Brownies, Goblins and Leprechauns. Only slaves would be allowed to stay as long as they were being useful.

Traditional Messengers to the human world are not doing their jobs and are loved by children when they are supposed to remind them of the power Fairies hold. They should be scared of these Messengers so they do as we wish. These Messengers must be removed from power - starting with the Sandman.

We promise to restore power to the Fairies and ensure all races bow before us. We will destroy Fairyland and rebuild it bigger and stronger than before! All traitors will be destroyed and their heads displayed in the Market Square as a reminder to all other traitors. We will not allow the power of Fairies to be wasted anymore.

You have the cycle of one full moon to give up your thrones and surrender to us or suffer the consequences. If you agree to these terms place the attached gem into the Fairy Fountain in the palace gardens at midnight on the full moon...

WE ARE WATCHING

Nyx

"Who is Nyx?" asked Chloe.

"We truly don't know who wrote this message. They wrote it in the blood of a Unicorn, it is forbidden to harm a Unicorn in Fairyland. A creature must very evil indeed if they can harm a Unicorn in anyway" said King Blackthorn gravely. "We have checked all of our records and have not been able to find any living creature in Fairyland called Nyx. The name was thought to be bad luck so none of the creatures living in Fairyland wanted to call their children by a name which would bring bad luck".

The King and Queen had already sent some special guards to the Sandman's house to check he was OK and to stay with him until the mystery was solved. Unfortunately by the time they got to the Sandcastle, the Sandman was already missing and the Sandcastle was being attacked by evil creatures who worked for Nyx.

"Some of the rainbow roads are already starting to fade as there are fewer happy dreams and the magic is fading. Please Chloe you have to help us, we cannot trust anyone in Fairyland as we believe there is a traitor among us" pleaded Queen Rose.

"Peter is an old friend of the family and we trust him with our lives, he is one of the best magicians in the Kingdom" said King Blackthorn

"He has also taken a vow of honesty and loyalty in order to undertake this quest and help you save the Kingdom. We are also including one additional member in your party. His name is Daithí and he is a

Leprechaun, if one of the rainbow roads collapses his magic can create a temporary road for you."

Chloe knew from school that Leprechauns had the power to use rainbows, she was very excited at the prospect of meeting one of them and wondered if he would look like the pictures in her school books. "He is waiting by the fountain in the Queen's garden, where this note was found" said King Blackthorn. "OK, let's go, we have no time to lose" said Chloe" "Woof, count me in" said Raggie.

Peter led the way. Soon they exited the palace into a garden, it was beautiful and there were thousands of flowers and trees of all sizes and colours. There were some Cherry Trees in full bloom. A swarm of Flower Fairies worked in the gardens keeping the plants happy and healthy. In the middle of the garden stood a beautiful fountain and as the water cascaded from the top of the fountain tiny rainbows shimmered in the water.

They could see a pair of shoes sticking out from beneath the fountain.

"Help! Help! I'm stuck! Can someone please help?" called a muffled voice from underneath the fountain.

Peter said a few magic words and the person shot out from behind the fountain with a whoosh and some fiery sparks leapt into the air. The person landed in a flower bed with a THUMP.

"Oooops too much magic" said Peter. "Hi Daithí, sorry about that! Are you OK?" said Peter trying not to laugh. "A little sore" grumbled Daithí as he climbed out of the flowerbed picking flowers and dirt out of his hair. Three Flower Fairies flew over to fix the flower bed which was squashed when Daithí crash landed.

"This is Chloe and Raggie" said Peter "they are here to help us find the Sandman and save Fairyland". "Pleased to meet you" said Daithí "let's get to work". "What exactly were you doing under the fountain?" asked Chloe giggling as there were still some flowers and a worm in Daithí's hair.

"I was looking for clues, when I somehow got stuck" said Daithí.

Raggie lowered himself to the ground and wriggled under the fountain. There came the muffled sound of a growl and them Raggie backed out from under the fountain and had a green piece of cloth in his mouth.

"Woof, it smells funny under there" barked Raggie.

Chloe took the cloth from Raggie. It was green and looked like it had been torn off by accident.

"Can you tell us anything about this piece of cloth?" Chloe asked Peter and Daithí. "Hmm it seems to be from a waterproof cloak. I am not sure from which of the Fairyland regions though. I know someone we can ask" said Peter.

"Can you follow the smell Raggie?" asked Chloe, "I would like to know where it came from". Raggie stuck his head under the fountain again "Woof, it smells like fish" barked Raggie.

He put his nose to the ground and started following an invisible trail which only he could smell. Raggie led them across the palace gardens, across a stream on a rainbow bridge and around the Cherry Trees. Raggie ran out of the palace garden and into an orchard. Chloe had never seen an orchard like this one. It had lots of different types of fruit from Avocado Trees to Orange Trees and strawberry plants. There were some fruit she did not even recognise, she made up her mind that she would come back when she had more time. Raggie raced through the orchard with his nose to the ground and soon they entered a beautiful rose garden. Many of the flowers were in bloom – there were red ones and white ones and some of them were even yellow with pink spots. It was truly beautiful.

Raggie stopped at a white rose bush and started wagging his tail.

"That is a lovely bush Raggie but we are trying to see where the smell goes" said Chloe.

"Woof, it ends here" barked Raggie.

Peter said a few magic words and the thorns on the rose bush disappeared.

"Those thorns will only be gone for a little time Chloe so you need to be in and out quickly" said Peter.

Chloe carefully stepped into the rose bush. The smell of the flowers was lovely, but she could also smell something not quite so pleasant. Near the back nestled between two large roots Chloe saw a bundle of cloth. As she reached for it she heard Peter shouting in panic "Quick Chloe come out someone has put a spell on this bush and the thorns are growing faster and bigger than before!"

"I can see it" said Chloe "just give me a few more seconds".

As she grabbed the bundle she saw huge, sharp thorns growing quickly all around her. She was terrified she was going to be cut by them. Suddenly she felt herself flying backwards. She landed on something soft, squishy and furry she realised Raggie had jumped into the rose bush and pulled her out to safety. She gave Raggie a big hug and a scratch behind the ears.

"Thank you Raggie, you saved me" said Chloe.

"Look! I got the bundle, I wonder what is in it" said Chloe as she reached for the bundle. "Don't open it here" said Daithí, "it could be booby trapped! Someone went to a lot of trouble with that rose bush trying to make sure it would never be found. It is a good thing that Peter is good at magic".

Daithí opened sack that had suddenly appeared. "This will contain the magic until it is safe to open this bundle" he said.

Chloe placed the bundle in the sack and with a shake of his hands Daithí made the sack disappear.

"Where has it gone?" asked Chloe curiously.

"The magic sack is linked to a room in the palace, it is shielded from outside magic and only the King and Queen know its location" said Peter.

"Don't worry it is perfectly safe. The King and Queen will examine the bundle and let us know what they find out."

"We have done all we can do here for now" said Chloe

"Where was the Sandman last seen?"

"At home in the Sandcastle" said Peter

"We should go there then" said Chloe.

Peter led the way back to the crystal dome. In the dome there was a crystal table on which rested four packages. Each package had a name on it.

"There is one for each of us" said Chloe "here is mine and look Raggie here is yours". Inside each of the packages was a shining crystal.

"Wow" said Daithí "these are royal Fairy stones there are only 10 of these in existence. Two were lost 15,000 years ago; no one knows what happened to them. These are very special" said Daithí. Chloe's, Peter's and Daithí's were on beautiful rainbow ribbons and Raggie's was on a dog collar.

There was a note on the table

These Fairy stones are a gift from us to you. They will grant you authorisation to travel safely throughout Fairyland. They will also allow you to communicate with us in an emergency. You need to hold them and call out in your mind for us. Be careful how you use it as others can hear your call and will know where you are.

Go with our love and be safe.
Queen Rose and King Blackthorn

Chloe hung her Fairy stone around her neck, as did Peter and Daithí. Then she carefully fastened the Fairy stone around Reggie's neck.

"OK, let's go" said Chloe.

They sat on the crystal slide, then whoosh off they went and were soon in the crystal dome of Fairyland Central Station. They descended the stairs where Iolo greeted them with a smile and a salute.

"Welcome back, we have been expecting you. If you need anything just let me know". "Thanks a million Iolo" said Chloe.

CHAPTER 3 – RUNAWAY CARRIAGE

They used the rainbow slide and whooshed down the slide to departures.

"We need to go to the main station in the Sandy Dessert and from there we can go to the Sandman's station" said Peter.

"Keep your Fairy stones out of sight for now" advised Daithí "we don't know who is watching".

Chloe, Raggie, Peter and Daithí went to the rainbow tunnel which had 'Sandy Desert' written over it.

"Last call for Sandy Desert today" shouted the conductor on the platform.

"Quick, jump on" said Peter. "We don't want to miss this one".

"I wonder why they are not sending anymore carriages to Sandy Desert today" said Daithí.

"This is very strange" said Peter.

"Why is it strange?" asked Chloe.

Peter explained that because there were many different types of creatures in Fairyland the rainbow roads were always open and carriages left from the main stations every half an hour all day and night.

Some of the smaller stations had single carriages that left on demand and the roads switched direction every half an hour to avoid collisions.

"You see" said Daithí "some creatures work at night and sleep in the day and some work in the day and sleep at night, so it's important to make sure all of them can travel when they need to".

The carriage lurched forward without any warning and started to slide along the rainbow at breakneck speed. As they sped away from the platform Daithí noticed that the conductor was still on the platform with a horrified look on her face.

"Something is wrong" said Daithí "the carriages started without the conductor!"

"What does that mean?" asked Chloe.

"The carriages should not be able to move without the conductor on board" said Peter. "The conductors are responsible for the carriages, they control the speed and the smoothness of the journey and this means there has not been an accident in 200 years" said Daithí. The carriage lurched sideways and they all fell off their seats.

As they picked themselves up off the floor they noticed that there were no other people in their carriage. "Where did they all go?" asked Chloe curiously.

"Woof" said Raggie "they were never here, I don't smell anything" barked Raggie.

Peter saw a red crystal on the floor. He bent over to pick it up. As he touched it there was a flash of light and Peter screamed and dropped the crystal on the floor.

Smoke twisted out of the crystal and in the smoke they could see a shadowy figure.

The figure spoke "I warned you Rose not to interfere. You will pay for your mistake with your life; Blackthorn still has until the full moon to decide. This carriage is out of control you have condemned yourself and your advisers. The carriage will not stop at Sandy Desert and you will crash into the station. By now the conductors know that they have a runaway carriage and will have evacuated Sandy Desert terminal. This will save innocent fairies. However the crash prevention magic won't work. Enjoy your last rainbow ride!"

The carriage sped on along the rainbow road and lurched dangerously as it followed the curves of the rainbow. "Why did that smoke monster call me Rose?" asked Chloe.

"I don't know" admitted Peter.

"Woof we have to slow this carriage down" barked Raggie.

"You are right" said Peter. "We will worry about the strange things the smoke monster said later". Peter looked out the windows and the landscape had changed, they were speeding along above a blanket of golden sand, which sparkled and shone in the sunlight. In the distance they could see a huge dome rising out of the sand and they could see all the rainbow roads coming out of the dome. If they hadn't been in such danger the sight would have been breath-taking.

"The carriages normally start slowing down from here" said Peter "it allows everyone to see the station and the beautiful colours".

Their carriage was not slowing down.......in fact it was picking up speed.

"The magic which is supposed to be slowing down the carriage is actually making it faster" shouted Peter in alarm.

Meanwhile Daithí was sitting quietly in the centre of the carriage.

"I think I have an idea" he said. "It looks like a reverse spell has been put on the carriage which makes it speed up when it is supposed to be slowing down" said Daithí.

"Peter can you do a spell to change it back to normal" asked Chloe.

Peter looked doubtful but he closed his eyes and spoke some magic words. A lightning bolt shot out of the red crystal knocking him backward with such force that he knocked his head on a bench and lay unmoving on the floor. Raggie bounded forward and picked up the red crystal in this mouth and dropped it out the window.

Chloe checked Peter. "He is still breathing" she said. Peter sat up with a groan.

"My head hurts" he said.

"What are we going to do now" wondered Chloe.

Daithí said "I have an idea, hold on". He picked up his shillelagh waved his hands in the air and said

"May the road rise to meet you.
May the wind be always at your back.
May the sun shine warm upon your face.
And rains fall soft upon your fields."

A rainbow shot out of his shillelagh and created a bridge between their rainbow and the one beside theirs. Their carriage lurched onto the bridge and glided onto the other road. "This is normally the outgoing rainbow" said Daithí. "I am hoping the spell was only on our rainbow and not the carriage itself. If this is the case we should slow down now." "Woof, woof" barked Raggie.

"We are slowing down, hurrah" said Chloe.

Just as their carriage stopped at the platform they heard a loud bang and saw flames on the arrival platform. It was scary and looked like their carriage had crashed. Chloe wondered what was on fire and what caused it.

"Hurry" said Peter "help me turn this carriage around! We don't want anyone to know we survived the explosion". They quickly turned the carriage around to make it look like it was ready to leave the station. The other platform was in flames.

"Come on we have to hide" said Daithí "The Fire Fairies are on their way, they will be here shortly".

"Wait" said a voice from the shadows "you must leave the Fairy stones here, throw them into the fire, Nyx must believe she is successful, the Fire Fairies will save them when the put the fire out".

"Who are you?" asked Chloe.

"I am a friend, you must trust me. Follow me I will lead you from here in secret and then we can talk" said the shadowy figure.

"Woof, woof, woof" said the figure to Raggie,

"Woof, trust her, hurry" barked Raggie.

They took the Fairy stones from around their necks and the one from Raggie's collar. Chloe took all the stones and threw them into the fire, the smoke from the fire started to change colour, and was soon all the colours of the rainbow.

"Woof, quickly, follow me" barked Raggie.

The strange hooded figure led them off the platform and down some steps underneath the rainbow road. The door had eight crystals embedded in it. The figure pressed several of the bricks in the wall of the station and as they did so each one briefly lit up and then the door swung open. Raggie confidently followed the person into the dark room beyond, he looked behind at the others and barked "Woof come in, it is safe – I promise". Peter, Daithí and Chloe followed Raggie into the room. The door closed behind them and disappeared into the wall. The figure pulled down her hood and they all gasped.

"Queen Rose" said Peter "Apologies - we didn't recognise you" said Peter bowing.

"It is OK Peter" said Queen Rose "My disguise would not have been very good if everyone recognised me" she laughed.

"How did you get here so fast?" asked Chloe curiously. "There is an emergency crystal slide underground from the palace to each of the main stations, it takes a lot of magic to use it because we cannot use the sun and the moon to give it power because it is underground. We use them very rarely and only when there is a real emergency" said Queen Rose. "It is one of our most closely guarded secrets. We have very little time but I need to explain some things to you. Blackthorn has already left the palace on the outgoing rainbow road to review the wreckage and recover my remains and those of my advisors" said Queen Rose.

"I will now share with you what we know so far, hopefully it will help you solve the case of the missing Sandman" said Rose.

Soft cushions appeared in the room and Chloe, Peter, Daithí and Raggie flopped onto the cushions. Trays of refreshments appeared on their laps.

"We received the bundle which you found in the royal rose garden" said Queen Rose. "It worried us that the bundle was so cleverly hidden and it was inside the castle grounds and we did not find when we searched the castle and the gardens. We opened the bundle in the safe room and discovered a cloak and a message crystal inside". "Excuse me, what is a message crystal?" asked Chloe. "A message crystal is a special crystal on which you can record a message. The message can then be played at a certain time or when certain circumstances are met" said Queen Rose. "These crystals cannot transmit images or sound, they just play the message" said Queen Rose.

"That is why the smoke monster called me Rose!" exclaimed Chloe.

"Exactly, the smoke message assumed I was on the carriage" said Queen Rose "I lent you my personal Fairy stone Chloe" said Queen Rose. "I am very sorry it placed you in so much danger. We do not yet know what is on the message crystal we have people investigating it" said the Queen.

She explained that the cloak came from a special workshop where fairies were looked after when they were sick. This particular workshop looks after Fairies that have been sick for a long time; the cloaks are then sold all over Fairy land. Certain cloaks were made for particular reasons. The Queen had sent one of her advisors to this workshop to see if they could tell which specific type of cloak they found and where it would have been sent. This would help them find the person who bought it and possibly the Sandman as well.

"We will allow Nyx to think I died in the explosion when the carriage hit the station" said Queen Rose. "This should allow you to move around more freely. Nyx does not know that you are looking for the Sandman. I was scheduled to visit a school here, so Nyx does not know it was you on the train" said Queen Rose. "This corridor opens into the back of a coffee shop beside the station; it is safe to exit there. You will be able to join the creatures outside the station that are waiting to use the station and get a carriage. Before you go please take one of these, Peter already has one."

The Queen handed them a golden gem. "This will prove that you have access to the Royal Palace" said Queen Rose "It does not protect you nor can you use it to communicate with us" said the Queen. "If discovered with the stone you will need to say you are kitchen staff or messengers, you should then be considered unimportant by Nyx and her followers, they should leave you alone then. If they check the details on the stone it will confirm that you have low level access to the Palace."

Just as the Queen turned to open the door that would lead them down a tunnel to the coffee shop a voice said "WAIT". They all turned in astonishment as they had not heard the other door opening. Raggie was sitting at the door wagging his tail. King Blackthorn stepped out of the shadows into the room. He strode across the room and hugged Queen Rose "I am glad to see you my dear" he said.

He turned to the others and said "As Rose has said the gems we have provided cannot help you communicate with us, so I am sending Lir with you". A beautiful parrot flew from the shadows and perched on Chloe's shoulder. The parrot was golden with hints of red, blue, green and yellow. Lir opened her beak and said "Pleased to meet you. I am bonded to Blackthorn and I can tell where he is any time of the night or day. I will fly to him with messages if needed. It will be slower than magic means but I will do my best".

Chloe clapped her hands in excitement as Lir's voice was musical and beautiful. "Welcome Lir, we are delighted to meet you" said Chloe.

"OK, let's go" barked Raggie.

CHAPTER 4 – SANDY DESERT

The adventurers walked down the corridor. It was very dark and gloomy. Peter created a magic light to show them the way. It was like a small blue sun and it bobbed along above Peter's head. When they got to the end of the corridor there was no door. They stood there confused and wondered what to do. "Are you going to stand there all day?" said a voice from the darkness. Everyone jumped back in fright, "Who are you?" asked Peter in a whisper.

Lir started laughing, her laugh echoed in the corridor. "That is not nice Petra" she giggled.

"Who are you talking to Lir?" asked Daithí.

"Why Petra of course!" said Lir in surprise. "Have you not heard of the doorkeeper?" she asked curiously.

Lir explained that Petra is the doorkeeper for the Royal family and that she is a magical creature who guards all secret doors for the King and Queen. "She loves making people jump." said Lir.

Peter moved his magical light towards the door and they could see a face peering out at them, grinning from ear to ear.

"Hallo" said Petra cheekily "What is the magic password?" asked Petra.

"Ermmmmmmmmm we don't know" said Chloe nervously.

"Petra stop playing games!" said Lir.

"I like talking to people, I don't get to talk to new people" complained Petra.

"Show Petra the golden gems" Lir said with a sigh.

They all took their gems out of their pockets. The room blazed into light. "You may pass" said Petra grinning. "By the way Peter, you didn't have to create a magic light - the gems work in any underground passage" said Petra. "Be careful when you use them as they are very bright as you can see, you could not sneak around using one of those" said Lir.

The door swung open silently. They waved goodbye to Petra promising to spend more time talking to her in future and entered a room in the back of the coffee shop. A beautiful Fairy came into the room just as the door faded into the wall.

"Don't worry" she said "Your secret is safe with me, I have been expecting you. Please sit down for a little while, my name is Meg and I am a fairy princess and Rose's sister. I own this coffee shop and I keep an eye on things for Rose. I discovered the Sandman was missing when he did not come in to collect his pancakes. He would normally come in first thing in the morning after his night working and get breakfast here. Pancakes, bacon and maple syrup every morning". "You must be hungry" said Meg. With a wave of her magic wand plates appeared in front of them.

"Just think of what you would like and it will appear" said Meg. "I am going to open the coffee shop now I will be back shortly. By the way, no one knows who I really am here so please keep my secret".

"Of course" said Daithí as he started eating his sandwich which had appeared on his plate. Peter had a toasted sandwich on his plate, Chloe had apple pie and custard, Raggie had a big juicy bone and Lir had a slice of apple and some seeds.

Soon the coffee shop filled up. Meg came back to their table.

"You can go now" she whispered, then in a louder voice she said "Thank you for your custom, oh my, a generous tip, I hope to see you soon".

Peter thanked Meg in return promising to come back as he had eaten the best toasted sandwich ever. The five friends walked out the door and joined the stream of creatures heading for the station. "We need to act normally now" said Daithí, "I know you will be a little scared getting onto another carriage, but Nyx does not know who we are so we are safe".

They went into the main station. The station was made of glass and they could see the Sandy Desert sparkling in the sunshine. There was a large part of the station which was blocked off and guarded by the Royal guard – they were all wearing black. Already many creatures had placed flowers and candles by the crash site. Peter gave each of them a white rose and they also walked past and left their roses. Iolo was standing guard and gave no indication that he recognised them.

They used the slide to descend to Departures. All the cushions were black. "Why is everything black?" asked Chloe. "Everyone thinks the Queen died in the accident" said Peter.

"Woof, this way" barked Raggie "We need to keep moving".

Daithí led them to the opening which had 'Sleeping Sands Village' written over the entrance. There were two goblins on the platform.

"Who are you and where are you going?" asked the first goblin.

"We are going to visit my sister who lives at the Sands Oasis" said Peter.

"We are conducting security checks" said the second goblin.

"Where is the conductor" asked Daithí.

"None of your business" snarled the goblin "turn out your pockets".

"What are those?" asked the goblin suspiciously. "They are access stones for the palace" said Peter "we work in the kitchen".

The goblin grabbed the stone off Peter and examined it carefully. "He is telling the truth" said the goblin, "he is probably too stupid to work anywhere else".

"You can go" said the second goblin.

They climbed into the carriage and waited for the conductor. Soon the conductor arrived on the platform; he too was dressed in black.

"All aboard" he cried.

Chloe watched the goblins jump off the platform and hide in the shadows as the conductor arrived. The carriage lurched forward and they slid along the rainbow. Chloe's fingers where white as she gripped the arm of her seat throughout the journey. They arrived safely at the Sleeping Sands Village station. This was a much smaller station and had only two platforms - one inbound and one outbound. There were four goblins at the entrance of the station.

"Come on" said Peter loudly "My sister's house is this way". They set off along a small path which was lined with palm trees. The trees are magic explained Peter, their job is to shade the path for all travellers. As they moved away from the station they saw some of the trees were dying and some were completely gone. "The magic is starting to fade" said Daithí, "we need to find the Sandman as quickly as possible".

"Woof" said Raggie "someone is following us, I think it is two of the goblins from the station".

The five friends stayed on the path for another hour and Raggie suddenly barked "They have turned back".

Lir took off and flew back along the path, she returned a while later "Raggie is right they are going back to the station".

"So what do we do now?" asked Chloe "We can't go back along the path to get to the Sandman's house".

"Don't worry" said Peter "My sister does live at the Oasis and she will help us get there, her house is not far." Soon the path opened out into a bowl shaped valley, in the centre of the valley there was a sparkling lake. There was a waterfall at one end of the valley which spilled water into the lake, as it did so rainbows shimmered in the spray from the waterfall. Around the edge of the valley there was a row of houses and shops. They blended into the growth cleverly so they did not stand out. Each building was covered in plant life and flowers like a living wall. There were animals in the valley and lots of colourful birds. On one side of the valley were lots of smaller buildings. They were visitor rooms and people visiting the oasis could stay there.

Peter led them to one of the houses, it was beautiful and orange flowers grew on the outside walls. A figure came running out of the house and ran across to Peter and gave him a big hug.

"Oh Peter, it is wonderful to see you. I haven't seen you in ages and you have brought some friends. Come in! Come in!" "This is my sister Sandra" said Peter. "We gathered she was your sister" laughed Daithí. "Really" said Peter "What gave it away"?

Sandra's house was beautiful, it seemed to be made of marble, and it had high ceilings and beautiful archways linking the rooms. Sandra said that the design kept the house cool all year round especially during the hot days. She explained that there was a magic force field around the house which protected it during sand storms or thunder showers. The force field also protected them from magical eavesdropping. Sandra was an undercover agent for the King and Queen in the Sandy Desert area. She also was a powerful magician like Peter. Peter explained that they needed to get to Sleeping Sands which was the Sandman's estate in the middle of the Sandy Desert. They told Sandra about the goblins at the station and how they could not go back that way. They asked her if she had another idea.

"I have just the thing!" she exclaimed.

She led them into the back of the house where there was a storage room.

"They are in here somewhere she said".

"What are you looking for?" asked Peter. "The travelling orbs, you know the ones" said Sandra as she had her head stuck in a pile of boxes rummaging through them.

Chloe was fascinated with the storage room. There were boxes stacked everywhere and strings of colourful crystals and beads were hung from the ceiling and sparkled in the sunlight. Peter said a few magic words and in one corner of the rooms the boxes started moving by themselves. Raggie started barking at them. Then the pile of boxes fell over and all kinds of things spilled all over the floor and three plastic objects shot into the air dislodging some of the crystals hanging from the ceiling. The plastic objects fell from the air and landed on Peter's head knocking him to the ground. Chloe and Sandra giggled at the surprised look on Peters face.

"They are a little bigger than I remember" he said sheepishly". "That is why I decided to look for them the usual way!" said Sandra

"Look at the mess you have caused".

Peter jumped to his feet leaving the travelling orbs on the ground "I can fix that" he grinned.

He waved his hands and said some magic words. "No please don't" said Sandra, but it was too late...

The things that had spilled on the floor rose into the air and started spinning around. They were flying all over the room. Chloe and Daithí we laughing, Lir flew up from Daithí's shoulder in fright and out of the room to safety, Raggie was barking at the flying objects wagging his tail and trying to catch them. Sandra sighed and watched her things fly around the room. The boxes which had been knocked over rose into the air and the things started flying into the boxes – neatly organising themselves. Chloe looked on in astonishment and said "I wish I could do that at home in my room - it would save so much time!" Sandra laughed "it is not over yet"

When all the items were in the boxes Peter clapped his hands to end the spell. But instead of floating gently down to the floor the boxes crashed to the floor spilling their contents all over the floor again.

"He never was any good at the tidying spells" laughed Sandra "never mind Peter, I will get the House Fairies to tidy this, they love playing with these things" laughed Sandra. Peter looked embarrassed and said "Sorry, I thought I had that one under control". "No problem you can help me get these travel orbs working" said Sandra "It has been so long since I used them, I have forgotten how". Peter clapped his hands and said "I remember" he picked them up and ran outside with them. Sandra winked at Chloe and Daithí as they followed him into the garden.

Raggie had run outside and down to the oasis, he was splashing around with some children in the water. Peter placed the three plastic discs on the ground a few meters apart and was inspecting them carefully. He waved his hands in the air and said some magic words. The air around the plastic things shimmered and they started to grow. In a few seconds the plastic discs were large plastic balls. They were transparent and there was one entrance in each ball.

"What in the world are they?" asked Chloe in surprise.

"These are travelling orbs" said Sandra. You climb into them through the door in the side and you tell them where you need to go and they roll off to that location. The orbs keep you dry and warm.

Chloe helped Raggie into one of the orbs and climbed in after him. Daithí shared one with Lir, and Peter and Sandra shared the third.

"Sandra knows the secret back entrance into the Sandman's house" explained Peter "so she is coming to help".

"Is everyone comfortable?" asked Sandra. "OK to Sleeping Sands please" she asked the orbs. The orbs started to roll across the Sandy Desert, Raggie trotted along inside the orb "Woof this is great exercise' he barked. Chloe has already fallen over and was sliding along as the orb rolled. She clapped her hands and laughed, she was having lots of fun. In the second orb Daithí had created a magic floating seat and was sitting on it looking around, Lir was perched on his shoulder. In the third orb Peter and Sandra floated in the centre of the orb chatting away.

CHAPTER 5 – SLEEPING SANDS

The Sandy Desert was beautiful. The sands sparkled in the sunlight. Soon they left the oasis in the distance behind them. In front of them they could see the most amazing building on the horizon. Sleeping Sands - the Sandman's estate - was amazing. The house itself looked like a giant sandcastle, but the walls were made of crystal which was sand coloured. To one side they could see several violet crystal domes. They were approaching the back of Sleeping Sands. As they approached the back of the house they could see rows of smaller houses arranged in neat rows.

The orbs stopped at the back wall and they all jumped out. Sandra explained that the houses they passed belonged to the Sandman's workers and that there was an oasis on the other side of those houses which the workers could use to relax and play. Peter waved his hands and the orbs deflated back to the small size they were originally. Daithí produced his magic bag and put the orbs inside for safe keeping. Peter explained that there still may be people watching the Sandman's house so it would be better not to leave the orbs out for anyone to find.

Sandra explained that the house itself was huge and underneath the house there were mines which the dwarfs operated. It was in these mines that the special Sleeping Sand was mined. The Sleeping Sand could only be found under this part of the Sandy Desert and was very deep and difficult to mine. Luckily dwarfs were excellent miners – they grew up in the Craggy Mountains and learned how to mine at the same time they learned how to walk. Many of them came to the Sandy Desert to work for the Sandman. Once the dwarfs extracted the sand from the mines they would put it into special carriages. These carriages would go to the crystal domes which were behind the main house. In these domes the Sand Fairies sprinkled the sand with magic Fairy dust. This magic helps humans sleep and dream happy thoughts. The happier the adults were the happier the children were and these happy thoughts keep Fairyland working and supplied the magic needed to keep the Rainbow roads working.

As they approached the back gate they heard a sound coming from the shadows "Psst, over here". A figure beckoned to them from the shadows. "Woof" barked Raggie, "it is OK, quick into the shadows". As they hurried into the shadows the figure raised her hand and blew gently towards the back gate. As they watched their tracks and footprints disappeared. "Shhh, keep still and quiet". As she finished speaking two goblins popped out from behind the trees on either side of the gate. "Did you hear that?" said one of the goblins, "No, I think you are dreaming" said the other. "I am bored, let's go to the oasis and cool down." The goblins left their posts and headed to the oasis.

They turned to the mysterious figure but before they could ask who they were Raggie had put his front paws up on the person's lap and was licking their face. The figure laughed and her hood fell away. It was Meg! "Hi Meg" said Chloe

"How did you get here so fast?" asked Peter curiously.

"A girl has to have some secrets" smiled Meg. "You can't go in the back gate" said Meg "they put a magic spell on it so they know when it opens then they check to see who has used the gate".

"How are we supposed to get inside?" asked Sandra.

"We need to go to the oasis, there are tunnels there which take water from the oasis into the mines and the Sandcastle for workers to use and for cooking and drinking" said Meg. "Not many people know they are there" said Meg.

Just as they were about to move out of the shadows Raggie whined and held Chloe back. "What is wrong?" whispered Chloe. As she said this the gate swung open and a giant came out of the gate. The giant strode over to the trees where the goblins were supposed to be hiding waiting for people going to the gate. He howled in rage when he saw they were not there "Where are you Fenrir, Hel get back to your posts!" bellowed the giant. Suddenly the two goblins came running from between the houses. They were wet and they were panting as they had run all the way from the oasis.

"Apologies Lord Loki" said Hel. "We just went to cool down" said Fenrir.

"Be quiet, you lazy goblins" shouted Loki. "You are supposed to stay here and watch the gate, King Blackthorn will not give up just because of an accident, he will send others" said Loki. "But there are no footprints and no sign that anyone has passed since we left for a drink" said Hel. "Do not leave your posts until I say you can" bellowed Loki "otherwise you will be sorry"

"Come on" said Meg "let's go while they are preoccupied".

Raggie led the way as he could smell any people or creatures ahead and could warn everyone when to duck into the shadows and hide. They had decided not to reveal their presence to anyone in case they were working for Nyx. When they got to the oasis Meg told them that the tunnels where hidden by a cluster of trees and plants so they would not spoil the beauty of the oasis. In order to get to the tunnels they would need to carefully crawl through the undergrowth and into the clearing in the middle. They kept to the trees trying to keep hidden. Then they crawled through the underbrush into the clearing. Even Lir had to walk along the ground as they were afraid that if he flew someone might see him.

They reached the middle of the clearing and looked around. It was beautiful. There were trees all around them and some of them were in full bloom with the most colourful flowers and some of them grew bananas and some grew oranges, lemons and even pears! Meg waved her hands and said some magic words. A blue light shone from her palms and expanded around them into the clearing.

"This is a magical shield" explained Meg "We can talk freely while this is working, I can only hold it for a short while so we need to be quick". Meg explained that after they left the coffee shop twelve goblins came in with the giant Loki. They ordered coffee and cake and Meg was able to hear some of their discussion. They didn't know who Meg was so she was able to listen.

This was how she learned that the back gate to the Sleeping Sands was guarded, she also learned that Loki knew King Blackthorn from his past and thought that he would still send people to investigate. So he was going to set a trap. Unfortunately she did not know the details. Meg managed to get to Sleeping Sands disguised as a dwarf who worked in the mines, she used the camel train which goes from the station to the workers house. Then she hid and waited for Chloe and the others to get there. She also discovered that the goblins and Loki had not yet been able to get into the Sandcastle yet. So once they were inside they would be able to search for clues. The goblins and Loki were in the grounds and were hiding at various entrances of the Sandcastle and the Crystal Domes waiting for the investigators to arrive.

Meg went to one of the trees in the clearing and took a red stone from her pocket. She drew the outline of a door on the tree and a door appeared in the trunk. Over the door a sign said "Water Works – No unauthorised entry permitted".

Eight crystals were embedded in the door, one for each colour of the rainbow and a clear one. Meg pressed a sequence of the colour crystals and when the clear one lit up the door silently swung open.

The passageway ahead of them had a river running along the bottom of it. The river seemed to flow backwards from the oasis. There were rainbow crystals embedded into the wall which lit up as they approached them and dimmed once they were past. It was a strange sight. Soon the corridor opened into a large room. The walls were golden like the sand from the desert and light sparkled off the walls making them shine and gleam. In this room there were pipes coming down from the ceiling, each of them was a different colour and on the wall there was a chart which explained which pipe went where.

- Black – water for the machines in the mine – recycles in the system before being pumped into the green holding tank
- Red – drinking water – filtered through sand and cooled before entering water system
- Green – useful water – recycled water from mines used for cleaning and cooking
- Yellow – bath and shower – heated by dragons, Fairy soap to be added once a day
- Blue – water for the crystal dome – triple filtered
- Orange – plant water – growth powder to be added twice a week

"We are now in the lower section of the Sandcastle" said Meg "We can access the house from here, we need to go upstairs" said Meg. They went to the door but it was locked. Peter stepped forward and put his hand on the door handle. He said some magic words and green smoke twisted from beneath his finger tips and into the lock. Suddenly there was a bright flash of light and a bang. Chloe was blinded for a moment. When she could see again she looked at the door it was still locked but Peter was nowhere to be seen. All that was left was his hat which was on the floor.

Sandra screamed and dropped to her knees on the floor. "Peter" she sobbed "I never got the chance to say how much I love you". The others clustered around her hoping to calm her down. Raggie licked her hand and put his head on her lap. While the Chloe and the others were comforting Sandra a voice from behind them said "What is going on here? Why is there so much fuss? Sandra why are you crying?"

Chloe spun around and shouted "Peter you are alive!"

"Of course I am alive" said Peter "why did you think I was dead?"

Sandra leapt up of the floor and knocked Peter down in her rush to give him a huge hug. Raggie bounded across the room and started licking Peter's face. Meg and Chloe started laughing at the sight. Peter and Sandra were sitting on the floor and Raggie was sitting on Peter's lap licking him. Sandra was laughing and crying at the same time she was so happy and so relieved to see Peter in one piece.

Daithí had turned to examine the door "still locked" he said "It looks like it is a magic proof lock. Lir flew over to the door and perched on the handle. He stretched out his claw and inserted two of his talons into the lock. He wobbled one way and then the other on the door handle and then just as Chloe thought he would surely fall off there was a loud click and the door swung open. Lir toppled from the handle but recovered and flew gracefully onto the now open door.

"Wow" said Daithí "that was impressive, you are useful to have around".

Lir puffed up his feathers and hummed.

"Lead the way Meg" said Peter. "Ok" said Meg "Raggie can you come up front with me and let me know if you smell anything strange?" asked Meg. Raggie wagged his tail and ran over to join Meg. The door had opened into a short hallway and at the end of the hallway was a spiral staircase leading to the main house.

CHAPTER 6 – THE SANDCASTLE

The corridor lit up as they walked along. The lights on the walls were in the shape of sandcastles and they lit up as they walked towards them and turned off when they were past them. The crystals in the walls sparkled in the light and almost seemed to move. The travellers climbed the spiral staircase which opened into a large room. The room had several doors. These included 'Deep Sand Mine', 'Sleeping Crystal Domes', 'Sandcastle House' and 'Oasis Entrance'. There was a timing device on the wall which looked like several hourglasses, there was a large top bulb with sparkling sand but there were three bottom bulbs and the sand trickled into them at different rates. Chloe couldn't help but stare at this contraption. "This is the centre of the Sandcastle" said Meg "Also known as the Hall of Doors".

"Where to first?" asked Chloe.
"Sandcastle House" said Sandra
"Fionn spends lots of time in the house when he is not working".

"Who is Fionn?" asked Chloe.

"Fionn is the Sandman" explained Sandra blushing.

"Why are you blushing?" asked Peter suspiciously.

"Well" said Sandra "Fionn and I spend a lot of time together when we can. He comes to visit me at the oasis when he wants to relax. He is a very good friend of mine" said Sandra "We can continue this discussion later; we need to start looking for clues now".

As they turned towards the door to the Sandcastle the contraption on the wall whistled and one of the bulbs lit up. Then the sand started moving backwards from the bulb back into the top bulb. Chloe was staring at it in fascination.

"Hurry" said Sandra "the dwarfs will be coming up from the mine any second now, that sound signals their break".

They hurried over to the Sandcastle door as Sandra approached it opened by itself and welcomed Sandra and guests to the Sandcastle. They hurried through the door and as it swung closed behind them they saw a line of dwarfs emerging from the door to the Deep Sand Mine, they crossed the hallway and started running out the door to the oasis.

As the door closed behind them a pixie ran up the corridor over to Sandra where she fell sobbing into Sandra's arms. "Oh Sandra I am so glad you are here, those monsters are trying to break into the house and Fionn is missing, I don't know what to do. I am keeping the house's defences locked but the magic is weakening without Fionn to renew it. What are we going to do?"

"Shhh Marie it will be OK I promise" said Sandra. "We are all here to help".

Sandra introduced Marie to the group. Marie was Fionn's assistant and looked after the administration of the Sandcastle, the Crystal Domes and the Deep Sands Mine. She had turned up to work earlier in the week and had been chased by the giant Loki. Luckily she managed to get inside the house and lock the door before he could catch her and force her to open the house. He didn't know about the hall of doors in the house that linked it to the oasis, mine and domes otherwise he would have used the dwarfs to gain access to the house. Marie and some of the other staff had been hiding all week as they were afraid to be seen around the house in case the monsters broke in. Luckily there was lots of food in the house and Marie had asked the dwarf leader to smuggle in additional fresh food every day.

"We need to look around for clues now" said Meg. "Please don't leave me I am frightened" said Marie. Sandra said she would go to the kitchen with Marie and talk to the staff who were hiding. Meg said that she, Peter and Lir would go and renew the Sandcastles defences with some magic. Chloe, Raggie and Daithí said they would start looking upstairs in the study. The main entrance hall to the Sandcastle was amazing, some of the crystal walls were like windows and the room was flooded with light which sparkled and danced across the crystal walls.

There was a huge staircase which wound around the room to the first floor. Alongside the stairs was a crystal slide which could be used when coming back downstairs, it was polished and shone brightly. Chloe couldn't help herself she ran all the way to the top of the stairs and then slid down the stairs laughing in delight. She ran back up the stairs and was going to slide down again but she bumped into Daithí. "Come on" he said there will be plenty of time for that later. We must look for clues". "OK" said Chloe reluctantly.

Raggie had run down the corridor and had his nose to the ground

"Woof over here" he barked. Chloe and Daithí ran down the hall to Raggie. "Woof do you smell that?" barked Raggie. "No" said Chloe and Daithí together.

"Woof, it is the same fishy smell we found in the palace garden" barked Raggie.

"Can you follow it?" asked Chloe. In response Raggie started trotting down the corridor with his nose to the ground. At the end of the corridor there was a door which was closed. Above the door there were hourglass shapes and they glowed gently.

"This must be the Sandman's study" said Daithí. Daithí tried to turn the handle but it was locked.

"Took you long enough to get here" said a familiar voice.

"Petra!" shouted Chloe in delight "What are you doing here?"

Petra explained that she had met the Sandman's doorkeeper Eve in the space between Fairyland and the human world. She was badly injured and had been hurt by Nyx when the Sandman was kidnapped. She ran away to the world between worlds in order to make sure Nyx didn't get into the Deep Sand Mine and the Crystal Domes. As long as she was not in the Sandcastle Nyx couldn't access the other doors. She was afraid she was too weak to withstand another attack so closed the doors and left. She was being treated in the otherworld by the Fairy Doctors. It would still be some days before she would be able to return and withstand the magical attacks from Loki and his goblins. Petra came to the Sandcastle in order to close the Sandcastle from Nyx and the other evil creatures. Lir asked her to stay and wait for them to help them open some of the doors in the Sandcastle.

"Why didn't you open the door from the waterworks?" asked Chloe. "Peter got hurt trying to open it by magic". "He should have known better" said Petra "I was making sure Loki couldn't get into the Crystal Domes".

"At the moment Nyx only has what little Sleeping Sand Fionn had in his bag. She needs to get into the Domes to get more and carry out her plan" said Petra.

"What plan would that be?" asked Daithí suspiciously.

"I overheard Loki explaining it to the idiot goblins he has guarding the back gate" said Petra. She explained that Nyx needs the Sleeping Sand as she plans to put all the people of Seree into a deep sleep and then she will take over the palace and control Fairyland. Anyone who does not agree with her or who fights against her will be put in a secret place where they will be made to sleep forever.

"Is that where she has the Sandman?" asked Chloe excitedly.

"Yes, but I don't know where this place is, Loki was very careful not to tell the goblins. I believe only Loki and Nyx know the location" said Petra.

"Well we better keep looking for clues then" said Chloe "please open the door". "Authorisation please" said Petra. Chloe and Daithí took their stones from their pockets and Petra opened the door. They entered a massive room. It was much bigger than expected. One side of the room were large crystal doors which opened onto a balcony. Chloe could see the Crystal Domes beyond the balcony. There was a large desk in the room and it was broken into several pieces with bits of paper scattered all around it. On the other side of the room the cupboards were broken open and sand bags and robes were strewn all over the floor. This was the first place Raggie went in the room. He followed the smell across the room one of the large cupboards. At the back of this cupboard there was a large sack. He pulled the sack from the cupboard with his teeth.

"This smells fishy" barked Raggie.

Daithí picked up the sack and emptied the contents onto the floor. From the bag fell a cloak with a hood, some boots and a mask!

"Nyx must have used a disguise to get into the sandcastle" said Chloe.

"It looks like the Sandman put up a good fight" said Daithí.

Raggie was sniffing at the cloak "Woof look here" he barked "there is some seaweed here. Daithí picked

51

up the cloak and examined the sleeve. There he found a piece of seaweed.

"I have never seen this type before" said Daithí confused "we need to send this back to Seree for examination".

Daithí was investigating the broken desk and found an envelope inside which was a piece of blank paper. He placed the seaweed in the envelope and wrote a quick note to King Blackthorn and Queen Rose asking them to examine the plant and let them know which part of the coast it came from. He wrote that once they were finished at Sleeping Sands they would head to the coast and that Lir could follow them. The first person they would visit there would be Fairy Godmother Susie. Daithí gave the envelope to Lir to keep safe.

"Let's keep our fingers and toes crossed for a good answer" he said smiling.

Chloe saw a red flash in the corner of the room underneath some papers. She crossed the room and moved the papers. There was a red crystal in the corner and it was glowing softly. As she reached out to pick it up she was knocked over by Raggie.

"Woof" barked Raggie "that looks like the crystal that hurt Peter on the rainbow". Chloe looked at the crystal and realised that it was a message crystal, but this one looked different it glowed softly. Raggie went over to the crystal and nudged it with his nose. Nothing happened so Chloe reached over and picked up the crystal, as she did so the crystal glowed bright red and then white.

From the crystal they could hear a voice "I don't have much time, my guest is not who she appears to be. I think I am in trouble. I have activated the Sandcastles defences. If I am taken from here the Sandcastle will lock itself and the Crystal Domes will lock and will only open for myself or Sandra. If anything happens to me tell her I love her. These people want my Sleeping Sand – they must be prevented at all costs as they are trying ....Arrggghhhh. Help me!"

Daithí came across the room and checked the crystal for the rest of the message. "It looks like the Sandman was interrupted and stopped recording".

Chloe heard a sob and she turned around. Sandra was standing in the doorway, she was pale and she was crying. "I miss Fionn so much" she said. "I want him back".

"We will find him, we promise" said Chloe.

Chapter 7 – Defences and Crystal Domes

Sandra came into the room and went over to the fireplace. She reached into the chimney and pulled something. A panel popped out from the side of the fireplace. The panel was shaped like a rainbow and had crystals embedded into it. Sandra pressed some of these crystals and as she did so they lit up. When she was finished, she pushed the panel back into the fireplace and stood back.

A section of the wall beside the fireplace silently slid open. They could see a short tunnel with a crystal door at the end. Sandra led the way down the corridor and the door at the end opened as she approached. They entered a circular room with no windows. The top half of the room was covered in TV monitors. There were many lights, switches and levels arranged on panels underneath the monitors. The monitors showed various parts of the house. They could see Meg in the kitchen with Marie and some of the staff, they could see the hallway where they first came into the house and the dwarfs were filling back into the mine for their afternoons shift. As they watched they saw several dwarfs leave covered baskets and bottles by the door to the Sandcastle. Four of the monitors had no pictures; instead there was writing on the screen "Emergency defence of the Sandcastle activated". There were some keyboards on the table.

Sandra went to one of the tables and sat down. She started typing, one of the blank monitors flickered into life and Chloe could see it was a computer monitor. Sandra explained that the Sandman knew that Sleeping Sand was valuable and he knew that there was a chance people would try to steal it. While he was in the human world he ordered some computers to supplement his magical defences. This was the main reason that Loki was unable to get into the Sandcastle. Loki managed to break the magical defences but could not figure out the computerised defences.

Daithí was fascinated as he had never seen a computer before, Chloe was looking at the screen and reading the information Sandra was typing into the screen. She was changing the settings on the defence network.

"What are you doing?" asked Chloe.

Sandra explained that at the moment only she had access to the house. She was adding Chloe, Daithí and Peter to the security system so they would be able to go to any part of the house. She was going to stay with Marie and the other staff and keep Loki out of the crystal domes. She wanted to keep Sleeping Sands safe and she was going to wait here until Fionn returned to Sleeping Sands. Meg was going to stay with Sandra and try to help her figure out who Nyx was.

Daithí asked Sandra if she could open the Crystal Domes as they wanted to look there for clues. Sandra explained that she could only open the crystal domes for one hour as the emergency defence system would not allow her to leave it open for any longer. Once the hour was up, the domes would be locked down and they would not open again until the emergence defence system was deactivated. As this could only be deactivated by the Sandman they needed to be sure they were in and out in the required amount of time.

Chloe, Raggie and Daithí made their way down to the hallway where Peter was waiting for them. There were several Sand Fairies with Peter, who had volunteered to go into the domes to ensure that the Sleeping Sand was properly treated and as a last line of defence should Loki manage to break into the Domes themselves. The Sand Fairies had rucksacks with them as they were bringing enough food to last for a long time as they were going to stay locked inside the crystal domes until the Sandman came back to deactivate the defence system.

The all went down the corridor and entered the Hall of Doors. They stood in front of the door which led to the Crystal Domes. One of the Sand Fairies told the group that the tunnel from here to the Crystal Domes was transparent and that if Loki was looking in their direction he would see them. Unfortunately the tunnels themselves were not magically protected and could be broken. They would need to be very quick.

The door silently swung open and Raggie peered out into the garden. It was strange the tunnel was completely transparent and gave the illusion that the person was walking through the garden. There was no sign of Loki or his goblins. The group ran out into the corridor and through the first section of the tunnel. As they approached the hedge that was around the Crystal Domes, Peter held up his hand. He cautiously peered around the hedge into the inner enclosure beside the Crystal Dome. There was no one to be seen. The group quickly ran through the last section of the tunnel and as they reached the door is swung open. They ran inside and the door closed behind them.

Once they were inside the crystal domes the Sand Fairies quickly stored their supplies beside the lockers on the right hand side of the door. Then they got to work, they flew around the dome checking the sand and moving some to one side of the dome, some to the middle and some to the other side. The Fairies on the right hand side of the dome were placing the sand into bags ready for the Sandman to carry. The ones in the middle were sprinkling the sand with Fairy dust and stirring the sand. On the left hand side of the dome the Fairies were moving the sand so it sparkled in the sunlight. It was an amazing sight.

One of the Sand Fairies had stayed with Chloe and explained that the sand was automatically pumped into the dome from the mine and that it entered the dome at the back through the rainbow pipes. The sand was deposited in the blue tanks at the back of the dome and the blue pipes brought triple filtered water into these tanks to wash the sand before treatment. Once the sand was washed it was placed on the left side of the dome where it was dried out by moving it in the sunlight. Once it was fully dried out it was moved into the centre of the dome where it was treated with Fairy dust to make it magical. Then it was moved to the right hand side of the dome where every grain was counted as it was packed into each bag. Each bag holds exactly 123,456,789 grains of sand. Since the lock down, the sand has been stored in the mines and they are running out of room so the Fairies need to start working with the sand again to make room in the mines.

Peter and Daithí were talking to the Sand Fairies about the sand and where it could be safely stored until the Sandman was able to come back and bring it to all the humans to help them sleep safely and have nice dreams. Chloe and Raggie were looking around the area where the lockers were. This was where the Fairies took their breaks and rested when they had time. Chloe saw a piece of paper sticking out from behind one of the lockers. The letter on the locker was 'N'. Chloe went over to the locker and pulled out a piece of paper. On the piece of paper there was a rough drawing of the Sandcastle and there were some numbers written in one corner. She showed this to the Fairy who was talking to Peter and Daithí, the Fairy gasped when she saw the paper and asked Chloe where she found it. This was a copy of the old security system in the Sandcastle and the numbers were the old codes which opened the

Crystal Domes, they now only allowed access to the main section of the Sandcastle.

Chloe pointed at the locker and asked who 'N' was. The Fairy said that one of her team Eoghan has been sick as he broke a wing trying to fly upside down and that a replacement had been sent by the agency to take his place. She was mysterious and refereed to herself only as 'N'. She did her job so the other Fairies didn't pay much attention to her. She had disappeared during the confusion following the Sandman's abduction. They had checked with the agency who had told them that 'N' had returned shaken but not hurt from the Sandcastle but would not return as she was afraid of being attacked.

"Can you please provide us with the details of the agency and of N?" asked Peter. "We will need to keep this piece of paper as well" said Daithí. Chloe suspected that the replacement Sand Fairy was Nyx and she was trying to get access to the crystal Domes.
"Why didn't she just take the sand while she was here?" asked Chloe. The supervisor smiled, she put some of the Sleeping Sand on the end of a long pole "Stand away from the door" she said. She extended the pole towards the door, there was a shimmer in the air and the pole and the sand were suspended in mid-air. "Try and move the pole" she said. Chloe grabbed the pole but she couldn't move it, Peter and Daithí also tried but couldn't.

The supervisor explained that there was an invisible shield in each of the domes and anyone trying to remove Sleeping Sand would be trapped in the shield and held motionless until the Sandman released them. The Sand Fairy pressed a button on the wall and said "Demonstration over - please release".

They heard Sandra in the background muttering "Trying to give me a heart attack are you?" Suddenly the pole dropped to the ground. The Supervisor explained that an alarm sounded in the Sandcastle when the shield was activated. She explained that any creature caught in the shield would be weak for several days.

"So Nyx would have to disable the security system before removing any sand" said Chloe. The supervisor nodded.

"We need help to check out the replacement Sand Fairy" said Peter. "She knew too much about the jobs the Sand Fairies do and too much about the Sandcastle" agreed Daithí. "Who can help us?" asked Chloe.

"We need to contact the Fairy Bureau of Investigation." said Peter. Peter explained that the Fairy Bureau of Investigation also called the F.B.I. was actually run by a human who had helped the Fairies many times in the past. This human adult was called Pat and was special. Pat could still see Fairies and was good at science and was able to help the Fairies investigate certain things. She knew human methods of investigating things and helped the Fairies combine magic and science. Unfortunately because Pat was an adult it was only possible to enter Fairyland once every full moon for only 24 hours. So Pat was not able to help them with this case. We will stop at the F.B.I. on the way to the coast and talk to Pat.

Daithí said "We had better hurry - our hour is nearly up. The supervisor said we can only open this door one more time before lock-down so you need to be quick". They opened the door and peered out and luckily they couldn't see anyone, so they ran to the hedge. Unfortunately they saw Loki in the garden with several goblins, they looked angry.

"They are coming this way, what will we do?" whispered Chloe.

"Woof, I will distract them" barked Raggie, "You run for the house".

"No way" said Chloe. But it was too late.

Raggie has opened a door into the garden and was creeping towards Loki and the goblins. "I will go with him" said Lir "close this access door behind me". Lir flew out into the garden. Just then Loki spotted Raggie

"Catch that DOG!" he bellowed.

Chloe, Peter and Daithí ran as fast as they could towards the house. As they got there the door swung open and Sandra pulled them inside.

"What about Raggie?" sobbed Chloe. "I have to help him".

"Lir is looking after him" said Sandra "Come and look".

Chloe followed Sandra into a room which had a view of the garden. Raggie was running around the garden and the goblins were tripping over each other trying to catch him. Just as they would get near him Lir would swoop down from the sky and peck them on bottom. Just then Loki grabbed Raggie's tail. Chloe screamed in fright. Lir swooped from the sky and pecked at Loki's face. Loki put his arms up to shield his face and as he did so let go of Raggie. Raggie bounded away. Lir flew down beside Raggie and then the two of them turned around and ran straight at the goblins. The goblins jumped out the way in fright. This made Loki very angry. Raggie and Lir went behind a bush and disappeared. "Where are they gone?" asked Chloe "are they OK?"

Chloe was not the only one confused the goblins were running around the bush and poking it trying to find out where the dog and the bird went. Loki was very angry he was stamping his feet and waving his fists in the air. Peter and Daithí also looked on in amazement. Sandra came running into the room. She looked delighted.

"I did it!" she exclaimed "I opened one of the air shafts into the mine. Raggie and Lir fell into the mine so they are safe from Loki."

"Where exactly are they in the mine?" asked Peter.

Sandra went red and stammered "I don't know exactly".

"We will have to go into the mine then" said Chloe. They agreed that Chloe, Peter and Meg would go into the mine. Daithí would stay in the Sandcastle with Sandra and make sure that Loki and his goblins did not break into the Sandcastle or the Crystal Domes.

Chapter 8 – The Sand Mine

Chloe, Peter and Meg entered the Hall of Doors. They were met by King Gordo who was the king of the dwarfs. King Gordo worked closely with the Sandman to mine the Sleeping Sand. He was very proud of his mine and the way it worked. His wife Queen Lizzie made sure that everyone knew what they were doing and where they were going. She was very organised and knew where everyone was mining where they were at all times. Queen Lizzie had noticed that one of the shafts opened briefly in section 13 of the mine. It was an old section and there were no miners in that section. King Gordo offered to bring them to section 13. Meg decided to stay with Lizzie to talk to her about security as Loki and his goblins were still trying to break into the mine in the hope that they could take the Sleeping Sand if they could get some of the special sand.

King Gordo warned Chloe and Peter that the old part of the mine may not be 100% safe so they needed to be careful and they should stick close to him at all times. They were give funny purple hardhats with lights on top to help them see where they were going. They would have to pass through the main shaft and through sections 3, 6 and 9 before reaching section 13. They walked down a short tunnel and through an opening. Chloe and Peter stopped in amazement. The main shaft was huge. There were 8 lifts; two on each side of the shaft, each one could easily carry 30 people. Each lift had numbers on the side of it. Gordo explained that these were section numbers, each lift stopped at specific sections. In the middle of the shaft there were huge transparent pipes and sand was drifting upwards in these pipes. The sand was stored in huge rainbow coloured tanks on level 0 and was automatically pumped into the crystal domes when the sand in the tanks there dropped below a certain level.

King Gordo walked around the main shaft until he reached a lift with the numbers, 3, 21, 30, and 36 on the side. He rang the bell and the lift shot up the shaft and stopped at their level with was called level G. They stepped into the lift and Gordo pressed the button with number 3 on it. The doors slammed shut and the lift seemed to fall down the shaft as if it was broken and out of control. Chloe screamed and Peter went a little green, both of them floated off the floor and when the lift suddenly stopped they crashed to the floor in a heap.

Gordo looked a little embarrassed and said "Sorry about that, I forgot you had not been on one of our lifts before. They are very fast and it takes some time to get used to them." Peter said "I think I left my stomach on level G".

Chloe helped Peter get up and smiled "That was fun, where to next?"

Gordo led the way into section 3, the transparent pipe ran along the ceiling and at specific points had pipes leading into rainbow coloured boxes. Gordo explained that as the sand was mined it was placed into carts which ran on the tracks they could see on the floor. When the cart was full, a dwarf would bring the cart to one of these boxes and empty the contents into the box, the box would weigh the sand and show the number of grains in that box. This number was written on a piece of paper and placed into a tube. This cylinder would be placed in the smaller purple pipes that ran along the ceilings. This tube would be sucked up by the black pipe and end up in Lizzie's office where this number would be checked against the number transmitted by the rainbow box. The dwarf would then wait until all the sand was gone from the box and it showed 0 on the side to show that all the sand was in the pipe and would then return for the next cart.

Section 3 was not in use at the moment so there were no workers in the tunnels. There was fireflies sleeping on the ceiling and their gentle glow lit up the corridor. There were also some clear crystals embedded in the walls which seemed to glow from the inside which also helped light the corridors. Gordo led them down the tunnel and at a crossroads led them down a corridor to the right, Section 6 was written over the entrance. Section 6 was in use and there were dwarfs with rainbow carts at some of the boxes. There were black troughs in the middle of the corridor which were filled with water.

Dwarfs with pickaxes were knocking pieces from the mine and adding these rocks to the black carts. When the black carts were full they were wheeled into the middle of the corridor where dwarfs ground the rock into small pieces before dropping them into the water. Some dwarfs were using nets to collect the Sleeping Sand from the top of the water. The wet Sleeping Sand was placed on a table where small dragons dried the sand before placing it into the rainbow coloured carts for counting. The dragons were colourful and they waved over and smiled at her as did all the other dwarfs as they passed by. Chloe wanted to stay and watch the colourful display as the sand was mined and the Sleeping Sand was extracted. But King Gordo kept on walking so she had to hurry to catch up.

At the next crossroads they turned right into section 9. This section was also busy but it looked older than section 6 and the corridors were wider. There were fewer workers here but it was just as colourful and interesting as section 6. They walked in silence for a while and then they came to a T junction. The sign for Section 13 pointed to the left. Section 12 and 13 were both empty as neither were in use at the time.

There were no fireflies on the ceilings and only the crystals on the wall glowed softly in the gloom. Gordo explained that these crystals stored light from the fireflies and this is what made them glow brightly in the other sections. As there were no fireflies in unused sections they could not store the light and so were dim. Gordo showed them how to turn on the light on their helmets. He explained that the Sandman had brought these helmets in from the human world to help the dwarfs explore the mines without carrying fireflies.

They turned into section 13 and the lights on their helmets helped to light up the corridor. The crystals on the walls glowed brighter as they approached. Suddenly they heard a terrifying sound from the corridor up ahead. It sounded like a giant was up ahead and was howling and banging the walls in anger. Peter, Gordo and Chloe froze with fear. "We should call for backup" said Gordo. "No" said Chloe, "They will be too late - we have to save Lir and Raggie."

Chloe ran forward up the corridor, the light on her helmet bobbing wildly as she ran. Peter and Gordo looked at each other and started running after her. Chloe ran up the corridor and rounded a corner where she stopped in amazement. Peter and Gordo nearly knocked her down as they caught up with her.

Peter burst out laughing and tears streamed down his face. He was laughing so much he had to sit down on the ground. Chloe was stuck to the spot and stared at the scene in front of her. In the middle of the corridor was a black trough from the side of it Raggie's tail was sticking out. Lir's tail was sticking out from the other side. On top of the black trough were two upside down Rainbow carts! They were jammed onto the black carts by some broken purple pipes which had fallen from the shaft. The banging sounds and howling sounds were coming from inside the Rainbow carts.

Gordo recovered from his surprise first and went to the middle of the corridor where he pulled the pipes away from the carts and pushed the rainbow carts. The carts fell off the top of the black trough with a bang and a clang. Lir fell out of the black trough and landed upside down in a Rainbow cart. Raggie stopped howling and looked over his shoulder. He was wet because there was water in the bottom of the trough. As soon as he saw Chloe he bounded over to her and jumped up and licked her in the face. Then he bounded back to the rainbow cart and pulled Lir out

"Woof look" he barked "look who is here".

Peter was still sitting on the ground laughing. Lir looked a Peter in disgust and then flew over to him and gave him a peck on the cheek.

"Thanks for rescuing us" said Lir "we didn't know what happened, we were running for our lives and then the ground opened up and swallowed us up and it was dark. We couldn't see anything then we were caught in the trap"

Raggie suddenly remembered he was wet and he shook himself showering everyone with water. No one minded as they were just delighted to see that he was OK.

"Let's go back to the Sandcastle" said Chloe "we need to find the Sandman".

Gordo led the way back through the mine to the main shaft. Chloe warned Raggie and Lir about the speed at which the lifts moved. They all made it safely to the ground floor where Lizzie and Meg were waiting.

Peter looked a little green, high speed lifts did not agree with him at all.

Lizzie and Gordo promised to keep bringing supplies to the Sandcastle and said that if they were need they and the rest of the dwarfs would help defend Sleeping Sands from Loki and Nyx. Chloe promised to return with Raggie and explore the wonders of the Sand Mine. She wanted to see where the light crystals were harvested and wanted to explore the rainbow rock section. Gordo and Lizzie walked with them back to the hall of doors and checked that the room was empty before they left the mine. The door to the Sandcastle opened and Sandra was waiting for them. They went into the Sandcastle. Sandra and Daithí were delighted to see that Raggie and Lir were ok.

"We need to get back to the station" said Daithí "We need to take a rainbow to the coast and stop at "Little Fish Ponds" to talk to Pat in the F.B.I. Sandra told them they would have to take the travelling orb back to the oasis and from there back to Sleeping Sands village. Once there they could catch a rainbow to the Coast and Little Fish Ponds.

Meg decided to stay behind with Sandra to help defend the Sandcastle against Loki and his goblins. Lir said he would fly back to Seree and get information from the King and Queen; he would meet them at "Little Fish Ponds". Sandra opened a skylight at the top of the Sandcastle and Lir flew out into the desert. Chloe, Peter, Daithí and Raggie went into the Hall of Doors and went through the Water Works door.

They descended the spiral staircase and entered the Water Works. They followed the sparkling corridor back out into the small clearing beside the oasis. The door opened as they approached and once they were outside, it closed tightly behind them.

They worked their way down to the edge of the Sleeping Sands oasis and when they were out of sight of the Sandcastle, Daithí pulled the travelling orbs out of his magic sack. Peter spoke the magic words and the orbs inflated. Chloe and Raggie jumped into one, Daithí into another and Peter into the last one. The orbs headed back across the desert to Sandra's house. Once they were there they took the path back to Sleeping Sands Village. There were no goblins at the entrance to the station so they entered.

"Where to now?" asked Chloe.

"Look for the rainbow to Sandy Beach" said Peter "It is the main station in the coastal area and we can catch a blue rainbow to "Little Fish Ponds" where the F.B.I. is located.

Chapter 9 – Fairy Bureau of Investigation (F.B.I.)

Chloe grabbed a pillow and slid down the rainbow slide to the departures level. She led the way across the station to the tunnel for the Sandy Beach station. She could tell it was one of the main stations as the road was rainbow coloured. The conductor on the platform was telling people where to sit. "The rainbow is losing strength" he explained so we are trying to make the carriages as stable as possible. Can you please sit in the second carriage".

Chloe looked nervously at the conductor and asked if it was going to be safe.

"Don't worry" he said "we have been given some extra magic from Seree for the main rainbow roads". A while later the conductor boomed

"Last call for Sandy Beach – all aboard"

The carriage lurched forward and was soon speeding along. Chloe enjoyed the feeling as the carriage travelled the rainbow road. She looked in fascination as they left the desert area and passed into the forest area near the edge of Seree. Soon she could see the ocean on the right hand side of the rainbow road it was beautiful. After a short while they saw a huge crystal dome ahead which was the main station of the coastal area. Thankfully this rainbow ride was uneventful and they arrived safely at the Sandy Beach station.

From the arrivals level they could see the sparkling ocean and the beautiful sandy beach beside the station. There were some fishing boats on the ocean working hard and on the shore they could see children playing. There were Fairies, pixies, dwarfs, giants and mermaids all playing happily together. There were even some dolphins in the water playing with the children as well.

"Woof I wish I could go for a swim" barked Raggie.

"Maybe next time" said Peter. We have to go to the F.B.I. quickly.

They all grabbed pillows and took the slide to the departures level. There they found the blue rainbow which went to "Little Fish Ponds". There was no one on the platform not even a conductor. There was only one carriage at the platform so they got in and sat down. Without warning the carriage took off along the rainbow.

"Oh no" said Chloe "not again".

They all put their seat belts on and clung to the seats in front. Soon the rainbow plunged underground and all around them was dark. The carriage stopped.

Chloe looked around "Where are we?" she asked Peter.

"I think we are at the station for Little Fish Ponds" he said. Daithí explained that because there was an entrance to the human world from this station it was underground. Daithí took his golden gem from his pocket and it blazed into light. The station looked deserted. "Who goes there?" said a voice from the shadows. "Identify yourself immediately".

"My name is Peter I am here with my friends, we were hoping to see Pat at the F.B.I.". The figure stepped from the shadows and said

"Hi Peter, long time no see".

"Jack" said Peter "I should have known".

Jack explained that the magic was failing fast around Fairyland and the magic that kept the lights on in this station had gone out. Jack was Peter's older brother and was one of the most trusted pixies in the F.B.I. He worked closely with Pat. Jack explained that Lir had already arrived with a message from King Blackthorn and Queen Rose. Jack said he would stay in the station to help them find their way back to the outbound rainbow. Jack led them to a section of the wall. He took a magic stone from his pocket and drew an outline of a door on the wall and a door appeared. He pushed it open and said

"Pat is waiting".

Daithí went out first to see if the coast was clear. He beckoned once he was outside be called the others forward. Raggie and Chloe came out next and Peter followed. Raggie started barking and running around in circles.

"What is the matter said Peter?"

He looked around and Chloe was standing still with her mouth open.

"Will someone tell me please what the matter is?"

"Woof this is Granny Pat's garden, why are we here?" barked Raggie.

"This is where the Pat the head of the F.B.I. lives" explained Daithí.

The door of the house opened and a person came out. Chloe ran towards her

"Granny Pat, it really is you" shouted Chloe happily.

"Chloe, I have been expecting you sweetheart. Rose told me you were helping out in Fairyland". Pat reached down and scratched Raggie behind his ears. He looked very pleased with himself.

Chloe opened her mouth, but before she had said anything Pat put her fingers to her lips and beckoned her to follow. Pat led the way to the bottom of the garden where she kept a small garden shed. She opened the door and beckoned them all inside. It was a very tight fit as the shed was small and there were lawnmowers and tins of paint in the way. Once they had all squeezed into the shed Pat closed the door and took a golden gem from her pocket. She placed it on the door of the shed and suddenly the floor of the shed started to sink into the ground.

A few seconds later Pat opened the door and led them into the F.B.I. itself. They walked into a huge hall. The area was painted white and glowed softly. Large windows along one wall showed mountain views and strangely they could see Seree in the distance. Pat explained that the windows were not real that they were windows between the human world and the Fairy world. The windows were enchanted to show Fairyland and they could move the view to where they needed. It was like a giant crystal ball. As they were curiously looking at the view it flickered and went black.

"We don't know why that happens" said Pat "sometimes they go blank. The big problem we have is that we can't see anything in more detail we need to work on them to make them work better".

A gnome came running across the hall and handed Pat a folder "The results" she said as she ran back across the hall. "Excellent" said Pat "Follow me". They walked across the hall where there were 10 lifts. Each one had a round circle in the middle. Pat walked up to one and looked into the circle. As she did so beams of light shone out of the hole across her face. A voice said "Authorisation granted", the lift doors opened and they stepped in. On the wall of the lift there was a row of buttons, each one had a different picture. Pat explained that the pictures meant different things. The one with the cup would bring the lift to the canteen, the one with the flower would bring the lift to the garden where you could relax and the one with the microscope would bring the lift to the lab.

Pat pressed a button with a 'P' written on it. "Hold on please" said Pat. The lift suddenly lurched to the side and Chloe, Peter and Raggie were thrown to the side. Just as they regained their balance the lift started to plummet and they floated off the floor of the lift, just as suddenly the lift stopped moving and Chloe found herself on top of Raggie and Peter on the floor of the lift. Daithí was laughing and Pat was smiling.

As Peter untangled himself from Raggie he turned to Daithí and said "Thanks for warning us, I presume you have been here before?"

In response Daithí just grinned and helped Peter up from the floor. The doors slid open and they stepped out of the lift into an office which was very beautiful. The walls glowed softly and there was a soft thick blue carpet on the floor, in the corner there was a small tree which grew strawberries.

Chloe ran over to the tree "Please may I have a strawberry, Granny Pat?"

Pat smiled "Of course you can Chloe but be quick because the tree will grow bananas soon".

Chloe picked a big juicy strawberry and then turned around looking very puzzled "Did you say bananas?"

Raggie barked and ran over to the tree wagging his tail. Chloe turned to the tree and saw bananas growing instead of strawberries. Pat explained that the tree was a gift from the King and Queen and that it grew something different each hour of the day. It was particularly useful around lunch time when it grew a variety of sandwiches.

Pat walked over to her desk and sat down. There was a file on her desk, she opened it and explained that her staff had been trying to work out who 'N' was and how she managed to get a job in the Sandcastle. Two days before the Sandman was kidnapped one of the Sand Fairies broke his arm in a magical broom race. The Sandcastle asked the Fairy Works Agency for a replacement. The same day this mysterious Fairy N arrived. She seems to know what she was doing so no one was suspicious. Unfortunately the Works Agency had no record of anyone from the Sandcastle asking for a replacement Sand Fairy. Somehow the message from the Sandcastle had been intercepted and an impostor sent to the Sandcastle for two days when Owen was injured. Pat had sent a Fairy to get Owen's broom to see if it was enchanted, she was waiting on the report. The F.B.I. had checked hours of video footage from the Sandcastle and still had not been able to identify the mysterious 'N', her face was not clear on any of the pictures. She must have used some very strong magic.

Pat picked up a remote control and one of the walls in her office slid to one side.

"These are the clearest pictures we have. Do any of you recognise this Fairy?" she asked.

They walked across the office to examine the pictures on the wall. Unfortunately the face was blurry in all of them.

"We have tried using computers to enhance the pictures but it does not work" said Pat. Daithí and Peter both shook their heads and turned away from the screens.

"Wait" said Chloe "What about her reflection in the water?"

Pat turned back to the screens "Yes, why didn't we think of that?" She pressed a button on her desk. "Get Kevin up here now" she said. A voice said "Certainly Pat".

Seconds later the doors to the lift opened and Kevin tumbled out of the lift. Pat explained that Kevin was an expert in pictures. Kevin ran across the room "At your service" he said to Pat while curiously looking around the room. Pat explained that Chloe had suggested that it may be possible to get a picture from the reflection in the water from one of the pictures. Kevin turned around and shot across the room. He started talking to himself as he sank to the ground and opened a book he had in his hands. He started drawing on the book and as he did so the picture on the screen started changing. Chloe curiously looked over his shoulder and saw that the book looked like the screen and as he drew he could change the picture on the screen.

CHAPTER 10 – NYX

As they all stared intently on the screen a face started to become visible in the water. It still looked a little strange. "Woof" said Raggie.

"Oh yes" said Kevin and he flipped the image as it was backwards in the reflection.

The face became clear and everyone gasped, "She looks like King Blackthorn" said Chloe.

Pat turned to Kevin "These pictures stay in this room, restrict access. No one else can see these".

Kevin nodded and added a code to the pictures and then left the room.

Pat pressed another button on her remote control; a steel door came down over the entrance to the lift.

"This room is now secure" said Pat.

She picked up an orb from her desk and threw it into the air. It floated into the air and expanded until it was the size of a large beach ball.

"Establishing a secure channel" said the orb, "Connecting now".

The orb flashed red and then Chloe could see King Blackthorn's face looking at her from the orb.

"Is everything OK?" said King Blackthorn.

"Unfortunately not" said Pat, "We have managed to identify Nyx".

"This is excellent news" said King Blackthorn, "Why do you look so upset?"

"Nyx is actually Hod" said Daithí.

"No, it is not possible, she was banished to another world, there's no way she could have found her way back" said King Blackthorn.

Pat explained that Chloe had seen a reflection in one of the surveillance pictures which the F.B.I. downloaded from the Sandcastle and it clearly showed Hod. Blackthorn stared at the picture for a long time without saying anything.

Then he said "Keep these pictures to yourselves, we will have to think about this", then he abruptly shut the link.

Chloe was still staring at the picture, "Will someone explain to me who Hod is?" she asked.

Peter explained that King Blackthorn has a twin sister called Hod. When she was a child she hurt animals and other creatures and killed trees in the palace orchard. She was two minutes younger than Blackthorn and so would not inherit the throne unless something happened to him. She was not pleased with this arrangement as she wanted to be queen and on several occasions tried to kill Blackthorn. She nearly succeeded when they were sixteen; Hod hurt Blackthorn and left him to drown. Luckily for him Rose found him seconds before his strength ran out and saved him.

She nursed him back to health and when he was strong enough she returned with him to Seree to challenge the Princess. When her crimes were discovered she was banished from Fairyland to Limbo from which she should not have been able to escape.

Limbo was a world between worlds where Fairies were banished when they broke sacred laws. It is forbidden for any Fairy to hurt another and it is unthinkable that one Fairy would try to kill another. Fairies that break this law are sent to Limbo to think about their actions and to learn from them. In time, some Fairies are allowed to return to Fairyland and live a good and happy life. Some others are considered lost causes and they are banished to the inner depths of Limbo never to return. Hod was convicted to spend the rest of her life in Limbo, she was instructed to help rule there and to rehabilitate and help as many Fairies as possible.

As Peter was explaining this Pat had called the records office and asked them to track down any Fairy sent to Limbo in the past 30 years with the letters n, i, x, in their names and the current status of these Fairies. As Peter was finishing the story of Hod a tube popped out of a plant beside Pat's desk and onto her desk. She smiled at the look on Chloe's face. Raggie ran over the plant to see where the tube came from.

Pat opened the report. "There were only 8 Fairies sent to Limbo in the last 30 years with all three letters in their name. One is very interesting "Nadia Ida Xia" has vanished. She was passed as ready to return to

Fairyland by the committee but she did not report for release. The committee sent a request into Limbo for a status update and so far have been told she decided to stay and help other Fairies. Nadia's family are concerned as she was passed ready to leave after 1 year and her daughter's 2nd birthday is in two weeks and she was excited about being at home for the event".

"Someone has to go and look for Nadia" said Chloe "she could be hurt". "I agree" said Pat "I will organise it however your priority is to find the Sandman and stop Hod from carrying out her plan. You must never refer to her as Hod outside this room, this information stays between us"

Pat pressed a button on her desk and the steel door slid back into the wall. "Come on" she said "we have one more stop before you need to continue your quest".

They all walked into the lift and Pat pressed a button with a fern leaf. This time everyone held on as the lift rocketed down through the building and shot sideways until they reached their destination.

CHAPTER 11 – F.B.I.
RESEARCH DIVISION

The doors opened and Chloe clapped her hands and ran out into the garden in delight. Everywhere there were beautiful plants and flowers. There were more magic fruit trees each one slightly different - some of them had leaves and flowers that changed colour.

"This is the reception area of our research division" said Pat. "They like to show off, follow me".

Pat walked across the garden to a waterfall, she walked directly under it and disappeared. Chloe ran after her with Raggie close behind. Chloe disappeared behind the waterfall. She stuck her head back through the waterfall and called to Peter

"Come on, you won't get wet, it's not real".

Peter and Daithí followed Chloe, Pat and Raggie under the waterfall. Behind the waterfall was a large room divided into glass rooms where various investigations and experiments were taking place. It was very interesting to see the creatures working in the glass rooms, they took no notice of the visitors as they worked. Pat led them through the maze of rooms to a large one full of microscopes and other scientific equipment.

"This is my own lab" said Pat, "I prefer human methods of investigation."

Pat switched on large microscope and one of the screens on the wall lit up. "Lir just arrived from Seree with the plant you found, we are about to examine it" said Pat.

Lir was perched on the back of a chair happily eating a peach. His beak was full so he waved his wings at them and squawked. Chloe ran over to him and gave him a big hug.

"I am glad you are safe" she said "I was worried about you."

Lir was about to reply when Raggie jumped up and gave him a lick on the beak. Lir beamed and gave Chloe a kiss on her cheek.

Meanwhile Pat had taken the plant to a counter and had sliced off a section. She placed this under the microscope. The image appeared on the screen. Pat switched on a second screen and went to the computer and typed in some commands. On the second screen images flashed up and were compared to the picture from the microscope by the computer. Chloe was fascinated - she was starting at the screen watching the computer try to match the samples. Suddenly the screen flashed green and the word 'MATCH' flashed across the screen in black writing.

Pat went over to the computer and asked it for the details. The computer put the details on the screen:

Plant Type: Water based
Plant Name: Wasabi
Typical Location: Fresh Water – low volume
Notes: Sample contaminated with Pink Grass

Pat typed another question into the computer "Locations in Fairyland with Wasabi and Pink Grass" The computer beeped and a list of locations scrolled onto the screen. There were 20 locations where these plants grew together.

Pat pressed a button and a 3D map of Fairyland was projected onto the table in the middle of the room. The locations where these plants grew together were marked with a flag. There were ten locations in Seree itself and ten locations scattered throughout the water region. There were two red dots on the map as well in the swap region.

"What are those dots for?" asked Chloe pointing to the red dots.

Pat explained that the plants grew independently in those locations. Pat decided to send teams to each of the ten locations outside Seree where the plants were found together. She did not think that Nyx would be able to hide in Seree as Blackthorn and Rose had already searched the city from top to bottom when they found the note.

She asked if Chloe, Raggie, Peter, Lir and Daithí would investigate the locations in the swap land where the plants grew independently and bring back samples of the plants for their analysis. Pat knew that Chloe wanted to help and so she was sending her to the location that she thought would be the safest. Chloe was excited about helping to find the Sandman and agreed.

Pat led the way back through the maze of research labs and through the waterfall to reception. As they waited for the lift Chloe looked around and said "Where is Raggie?" Suddenly Raggie burst out from behind the waterfall with three F.B.I. agents close behind.

"Woof Woof" he said. Chloe started laughing. Raggie was green from his nose to the tip of his tail!

"What happened?" asked Chloe.

The angry F.B.I. agents started yelling. "That dog ate our new experimental biscuit and now it's gone! Look he has turned green. He will be taken into custody for interfering with a Federal experiment!" The angry agents grabbed Raggie and started to pull him back towards the waterfall.

Chloe started to cry as she was frightened for Raggie "Granny Pat do something" she pleaded.

"Enough" said Pat "leave the dog here. If anything he has proven that your biscuit needs work. The subject should turn invisible not green if I remember correctly".

One of the agents turned around

"Who do you think you are? Telling us what to do."

He noticed that the other agents had let go of Raggie and they looked very sorry.

"What are you two doing?" he snarled "Help me with this beast!"

Pat stepped forward

"I said enough, put the dog down and get back to work!"

The third agent turned around, when he saw who spoke he went pale.

"Sorry Sir I didn't see you there" he stammered.

Pat made a note in her notepad and said

"I will be carrying out an audit of your security procedures later this week. I also want a full report on the issues relating to your disappearing biscuit experiment. By the way how long will the dog be green?" asked Pat.

"It shouldn't last any more than 10 hours" stammered one of the agents "we are working on a reversal biscuit, but that doesn't work that well either at the moment" she said quietly.

"Well don't just stand there" said Pat "Back to work".

Raggie was sitting down with a big dog grin on his face

"Woof that was a lovely biscuit, can I have another?"

"No you can't" said Chloe "Look you are green".

Peter and Daithí were laughing and Lir was flapping his wings trying not to laugh.

Pat sighed

"Let's get you out of here before something else happens" she said.

They all got into the lift and Pat pressed the button that looked like a fish pond.

"This will bring you to an entrance in my garden" she said "then you can go back to the station. Jack will show you where to go – give him this" said Pat as she handed Peter a scroll tied in red ribbon.

The lift stopped and they all got out except for Granny Pat. She gave Chloe a big hug and said "You be careful and be safe" she turned to the Raggie who was surprisingly hard to see when he lay on the grass "You look after my little granddaughter or no more biscuits for you!" she said.

Peter led the way to the bottom of the garden and drew a door on one of the trees. As they stepped into the darkness they heard Jack "Who goes there? Oh it's you!"

Peter gave Jack the scroll, a while later Jack said "Come on guys, follow me." Jack led them through the dark station which was only lit up by dim blue crystals in the walls.

"Be careful here" he said "there are some steps".

He led them up the steps and down a corridor – he opened a door to the next section of the station and a bright light shone through the door.

"Quickly, come out here" said Jack. Once they were all through the door he closed it behind them.

When Chloe turned around she could see no trace of the door. "Where are we?" she asked curiously.

Jack explained that he had led them through the service tunnel to another station called Sandy Beach. Pat thought that the carriages from Little Fish Ponds were being monitored so she asked Jack to bring them to this station which was very close but only the F.B.I. knew of the passages from one to the other.

"You need to go to the Bog of Frogs" he said. ":Let's find the right rainbow".

They went down the slide to Departures and found the rainbow departing for the Bog of Frogs.

"You have tickets for carriage number 5" said jack "Sit on bench 7, when the carriage is moving look under your seat. Best of luck now, enjoy your holiday!"

Chloe turned around to say thank you to Jack, but he had vanished. She looked around in confusion but Jack was nowhere to be seen.

Chapter 12 – Bog of Frogs

Chloe, Raggie, Peter, Daithí and Lir got onto the carriage just as the conductor was calling for the last remaining passengers. They took their seats as the carriage moved away from the platform along the rainbow. Chloe reached under the seat and found a bag with her name on it. She curiously opened the bag and found a note from Granny Pat.

"I have added some food to this bag as well as information and maps for your journey. There are two magic bags for transporting the plants directly back to the FBI – simply place the items in the bags and say 'As Láthair' and this will send the samples back to us, then you can catch the next rainbow back to Seree". Once Chloe read the message the paper magically dissolved and blew away.

Chloe reached into the bag and found a map of the Bog of Frogs with the two locations clearly marked. There were walking directions to both locations. Inside there was an empty box for each of them with their names on them.

"What are these?" asked Chloe curiously.

Daithí grabbed his and said "Oh wow, oh wow, oh wow! I have always wanted one of these!"

Chloe was still holding hers wondering what was so exciting about an empty box.

Peter took his box. "Watch me" he said. Peter held his box so the lid was facing up and said "Ba mhaith liom Chicken Sandwich" the box started to glow and then there was a Chicken Sandwich in the box. Peter took the lid off and took a bit bite of his sandwich "Delicious" he exclaimed happily.

Daithí had already asked for a slice of chocolate cake and was happily munching away. Lir asked for a sesame seed cake and Raggie was chomping on a bone. Chloe held her box in her hands and thought for a while "Ba mhaith liom Cheese, ham and tomato sandwich" her box glowed brightly and then her sandwich appeared. It was one of the best sandwiches she had ever eaten. Once she finished the sandwich she asked for chocolate cake and that was the best chocolate cake in the world. As they finished their lunches the carriage pulled into a platform which was on one the side of the rainbow. They jumped out quickly and the carriage continued on its way.

Chloe looked into the bag and at the bottom of the bag there was a glass egg. There was red writing on the egg 'Break in case of emergency' Chloe carefully lifted the egg from the bag. Raggie sniffed at it curiously.

"We'd better put this in a safe place" said Chloe.

They put the magic lunchboxes back into the bag. Daithí took the map. Chloe put the glass egg in her pocket for safe keeping. Daithí and Peter were arguing over the map each pointing in a different direction. Lir swooped down from his perch and grabbed the map. He turned it the right way up and pointed to a small path which led away from the platform.

The path was very narrow and they had to walk in single file. It looked like some people had been down the path recently. Wooden bridges kept the path off the wet bog land. Soon the path opened into the Bog of Frogs – it was huge and all Chloe could see was a sea of rushes with small islands of dry land sticking up from the bog in places. They were at the edge of the bog. In front of them wooden walkways spread out over the bog connecting the little islands to each other. "We need to be careful" said Peter. "Fairies have been known to get lost in here and have never been seen again!"

Lir was looking at the map. He flew down and perched on Chloe's shoulder, "We need to go to this island first because that is where the pink grass grows". With Lir leading the way, the small group of friends made their way further into the Bog of Frogs. It was a maze of walkways, occasionally Chloe could see large fish swimming under the walkways, they had sharp teeth and Chloe wondered if they would eat her if she fell in.

They finally arrived at the island with the pink grass - it was beautiful. It was covered in grass but this grass was pink – there were some little frogs hopping around the island. They were very easy to see because they were green and the grass was pink. Raggie rushed around excitedly trying to pounce on a frog. He looked like a giant furry frog as he was green as the effects of the biscuit had not yet worn off.

Peter took a mini shovel out of the bad and dug up a small patch of the pink grass and placed it carefully in one of the magic bags.

"As Láthair" he said and the bag vanished along with the sample of pink grass.

"One down, one to go' he said. Raggie had flopped down onto the grass as he was tired from chasing frogs. He lay there panting, his pink tongue hanging out! Daithí gave him some water while Lir and Peter were studying the map.

Once again they set out across the bog with Lir leading the way. On one of the paths they came to a broken bridge.

"This is the only way across" said Lir.

"What are we going to do?" asked Chloe.

"Woof, something smells funny" said Raggie. He put his nose to the ground and started following a smell.

Chloe screamed "Raggie stop!"

Raggie stopped and turned around looking puzzled "Woof, follow me" he said.

"Look down" said Peter.

Raggie looked down and to his astonishment could not see anything underneath him although his feet told him he was still on the bridge. Daithí slowly walked to the edge of the bridge holding onto the railing, his hand continued to follow the railing into thin air. "Someone has gone to a lot of trouble to make this bridge appear broken" he said "it has been made invisible!"

"I have a bad feeling about this" said Lir "We should go back".

"No" said Chloe "Granny Pat asked us to find that plant and that is what we are doing"

Lir decided he should fly back to the F.B.I. and report the invisible bridge in case it caused an accident. He waved goodbye to his friends and took off towards the coast. Raggie continued across the bridge onto an island which had a huge clump of the Wasabi plant growing beside the bridge. "That is where the funny smell was coming from" said Chloe wrinkling her nose. Raggie ran to the other side of the island to be as far away from the smell as possible. Once he was lying still he was very hard to see because he was still green. Peter took out his little shovel again and placed it into the magic bag.

Just as the bag disappeared there was a loud bang and three goblins appeared along with Loki the giant.

"Well, well, well, what do we have here?" growled Loki.

"You three again! Haven't you stopped causing trouble yet? You shouldn't have come here"

Raggie started to growl but Chloe motioned him to lie back down as the goblins hadn't seen him yet.

One of the goblins started laughing "Can we throw them into the bog? he asked in a squeaky voice.

"No" said Loki "these will be useful, Blackthorn will be very unhappy we captured these helpers as well."

As he spoke another goblin came onto the island from another bridge and he dragged a net behind him with Lir in the net. Lir looked very sad. Two more goblins came from another bridge, Loki turned to them "Did you find the dog?" he growled.

"He is not here" said the other goblins.

"Ok" said Loki "tie those three up and bring them to the hideout. The boss will be very interested in them."

Before the goblins could tie Chloe up she reached into her pocket and threw the glass egg as hard as could onto the ground. A star shot out of the egg and flew high into the air getting brighter and brighter as it got higher! Loki took out a crossbow and shot the star, it shattered into thousands of pieces and blew away on the wind.

"Nice try! Keep an eye on that one - she is trouble" he said.

The goblins roughly tied everyone's hands behind their backs and pushed them towards one end of the island and onto another invisible bridge! Raggie stayed where he was for a while, afraid to move. Seconds before he moved he heard a POP! And a figure suddenly appeared from nowhere. It was Nyx. She was talking to herself

"Well I guess they weren't being followed. I wonder how they found me! I need to talk to my friend in the F.B.I."

Nyx continued to talk to herself as she walked across the invisible bridge towards her hideout.

Raggie was about to follow when he noticed the bag Pat gave them had been thrown in a heap beside a tree; he suspected Peter threw it there. There was a voice coming from the bag. "Agent in distress. Please report".

Raggie stuck his head inside the bag and found a communication crystal.

"Woof they have taken Chloe and the others" said Raggie.

"Who have taken them and to where?" asked a worried Pat.

"Woof, Loki and the other goblins have taken them, Nyx was here too. I am going after them" barked Raggie.

Before Pat had a chance to argue Raggie dropped the crystal and sniffed the ground. He knew what Chloe smelled like and was not going to let her get hurt! He followed the trail across two invisible bridges to a larger island which had lots of trees and then the smell vanished. Raggie was puzzled, he was sure the smell led to this place. Just as he was about to turn around and go back to see if there was another trail he heard someone coming. He ran over to some long grass and lay down to hide; he was very well hidden as he was still green. A Fairy came around the corner from another bridge.

The Fairy was talking to Loki angrily "How stupid can you be? They were just about to leave when you captured them. The little girl is working with the F.B.I. they will stop at nothing to find her. The distress beacon activated a communication crystal. The F.B.I. knows we are here and they will come after the little girl. Get the prisoners out of here and transport them into Limbo, they won't follow us there!" ordered the Fairy. Raggie was sure he had seen the Fairy somewhere before but couldn't remember where.

"They won't find us" said Loki confidently "We are a long way from the island where we took them. Anyway we can't go to Limbo. Nyx isn't here. She just left on a mysterious errand, she said she wouldn't be long. We will have to wait for her".

As Raggie watched they pressed some sections on one of the trees and a stair s appeared leading deep underground into the Bog. When they were out of sight Raggie ran over to the door but it slammed shut before he could get through. Raggie tried to open the door again but he couldn't. He walked around the island to see if there was another way into the Bog. The island was much larger than the other ones and had lots of trees which were perfect for hiding. Raggie searched and searched but he couldn't find a way in. He lay down on the grass and sighed. He was very sad, he was about to get up and go back to look for help when a little green frog hopped over to him.

CHAPTER 13 – RAGGIE TO THE RESCUE

""Hello my name is Fergus. Why are you so sad?" the frog asked "this is a perfect place for frogs to play you should be happy here".

"Woof I am not a frog. I am a dog and I can't find Chloe" barked Raggie.

"Are you looking for the nice little girl and her friends?" asked Fergus "The mean goblins dragged them past here some time ago."

"Woof do you know how to get to them?" asked Raggie excitedly.

"They have secret doors all over this island" said the Fergus "but you won't be able to open them, they locked them with magic and I can't open them either."

Raggie's tail dropped and he looked sad.

"Maybe you can go in the underwater way?" suggested the Fergus.

Fergus explained that the 'mean goblins' were using the old palace which used to belong the people from the Bog and was the home to the Duke and Duchess Frogs who looked after the bog for King Blackthorn and

Queen Rose. The secret doors in the trees were used by the land creatures and the underwater passages by the water creatures. About nine months ago the goblins came with some Fairies and took over the palace. They captured many of the bog creatures from the land and the water. They said if anyone told the Fairy folk then the prisoners would be sent to Limbo and would be there forever. Fergus was a frog prince the Duke and Duchess are his parents. He hid when the palace was taken over. He was able to get into the section of the palace cellars where the land creatures were held prisoner but had been unable to free them. He hadn't been able to find the water creatures or to help his Mom and Dad. He said if Raggie could help free his Mom and Dad, he would help in any way he could.

Fergus led Raggie to the edge of the bog and warned him he would have to hold his breath for at least 180 seconds. Raggie was worried but bravely agreed to follow the frog. He hoped the frog was on his side! Fergus led Raggie around the island to a section where trees grew straight out of the bog in a semi-circle. It would be impossible to get onto the island from here as the trees rose high into the air. The frog told Raggie to take a deep breath and dived into the water. Raggie followed, it was hard to see under the water but he kept up with Fergus swimming right behind him. Fergus swam beneath two of the trees, their roots had formed an archway under the water. There was a long narrow passage ahead, which Fergus swam down. Just as Raggie thought his lungs were going to burst they emerged into an underwater cave and swam to the surface of the water. Raggie lay on the shore gasping for air for a while until his breathing came back to normal.

The cave was glowing softly, Fergus explained that the mushrooms that grew in the cave glowed in the dark and lit the cave. He said that this area of the palace was not being used and none of the mean goblins came this far. He led the way along a ramp into a series of interconnecting tunnels. Fergus explained that when the palace was operational these passages were half full of water to allow the water creatures to swim into the palace. The walkways were for the land creatures so they could walk alongside their aquatic friends. When the mean goblins took over the palace they turned off the machinery that kept the water flowing so many of the water creatures could not reach the palace to check on their loved ones. The frog said if Raggie could turn these rivers back on, then the water creatures would be able to help the land creatures escape.

Raggie thought about it and said it would be a good idea but he would need help. The frog said that the mean creatures recently brought two dwarfs down into the tunnels a while ago and forced them to work making some of them bigger so they could capture more prisoners. He said that they were left locked into the lower tunnels during the day and perhaps they would help. The frog was afraid of them so he hadn't spoken to them.

Raggie heard banging up the corridor which sounded like dwarfs mining he ran up the corridor towards the sound, when he ran around the corner he stopped in astonishment. The dwarfs were none other than Gordo and Lizzie.

"Woof woof" said Raggie as he licked Gordo from head to toe.

"Raggie" cried Lizzie "It is you! Why are you all green? Have you come to rescue us?" "Woof one question at a time" laughed Raggie "Yes it is me, I am green it is a long story and I need your help to rescue Chloe and the others".

Raggie introduced Fergus to Gordo and Lizzie and explained the plan. Gordo and Lizzie explained that after Chloe had left the Sandcastle that he and Lizzie had left the mine to check that the vent which Sandra had opened to rescue Raggie and Lir was properly closed. Unfortunately they were caught by some of the goblins trying to break into the crystal domes and Loki brought them here by magic and locked them in.

They said they had seen the machinery but they didn't know how it worked. Fergus promised to show them how it worked so they could fix it. As they were walking through the tunnels towards the machinery Fergus described how beautiful the palace used to be and how King Blackthorn stayed with them when he was ill with Rose years ago after a fishing accident. He told them about the creatures both water and land who used to visit the palace and the games they played. He was able to play with the land creatures and the water creatures and had many friends. He had not seen most of them for a long time and was afraid for them.

Soon they reached the room where the machinery was dismantled and thrown around the room. Luckily it was not badly broken. Raggie stood guard at the door while Fergus told Gordo and Lizzie what the machine should look like. It took some time to figure out which parts went where and to figure out how they all fitted together, it was like a giant 3D Jigsaw. Once it was all together Fergus told them how to turn the machine on. Lizzie had to stand on Gordo's shoulders to reach the switch that turned on the machine. Once it was turned on they waited and listened for any sound to see if it would work. They could hear nothing

"Maybe they broke something else" said Fergus the Frog sadly.

"Woof, Woof, I can hear something" barked Raggie.

Raggie ran down one of the corridors and stopped at a dead end, the corridor was blocked by rocks. They could see a trickle of water making its way through the blockage but not enough to fill the corridors with enough water to allow the aquatic creatures.

"I can fix this" said Gordo proudly as he swung his pickaxe at the blockage

"No wait" screamed Lizzie... But it was too late!

Gordo had swung his pickaxe high in the air and hit the blockage as hard as he could. The rocks causing the blockage were suddenly loosened and they gave way suddenly. The water rushed through the gap pushing the rest of the blockage out of the way. Fergus, Raggie, Gordo and Lizzie were swept down the corridor as the water rushed into the corridors. Luckily for them they were swept along the top of the corridor they and were washed into one of the higher walkways which allowed the land creatures to walk beside the aquatic creatures.

All four of them ended up in a wet soggy heap in the corner of one of these corridor as the water rushed past them filling up waterways that connected the palace to the bog.

Soon the water slowed down and stopped. The system was full again and the water clear, blue and calm. Lizzie was hitting Gordo on the back of the head
"How could you be so stupid?" she shrieked, "you could have killed us all!"

She started crying and Gordo gave her a big hug and apologised to her. Fergus thought it was great fun and wanted to do it again!

"Come on" said Fergus "Follow me and we can release my Mom and Dad they will know what to do and how to get help for Chloe and the others".

Fergus led the way along the corridors until they reached a big wooden door. Gordo tried to open the door and couldn't. It is locked he said. Fergus jumped into the water and swum to the bottom of the door where there was a gap just big enough for a small frog to fit under. He hopped out on the other side and saw the aquatic creatures trapped in tanks. "Help us" they pleaded.

Unfortunately Fergus was not able to let them out of the tanks. They were being automatically fed from big tubes which were coming from the ceiling. These were usually used by the water creatures and allowed them to swim up to the higher levels of the palace. When the goblins came to take over the place the water creatures tried to use these tubes to escape.

However Nyx had placed glass tanks under them so all the creatures trying to escape were jumping into a large trap.

Fergus saw the spare key to the door blocking the corridor hanging on a big nail on the wall. It was very high, but he was sure he could jump to it and knock it down. He jumped and jumped and jumped but was unable to reach the nail. He was very sad and started to cry. His Mom and Dad called him over to their tank. They whispered something in his ear and slowly a big grin spread across his face. He started to run at the wall and just before he reached it he jumped onto the side of one of the glass tanks and bounced off it and up the wall to the key. He grabbed the key and swung below it backwards and forwards. He pushed his legs against the wall and suddenly both frog and key fell to the ground with a loud thump! Fergus was lying on the ground stunned for a few moments and all the water creatures were quiet hoping he was OK. Then he rubbed his head and sat up, the water creatures began to cheer. Fergus dragged the key back to the door and pushed it under through a very small hole. Gordo grabbed it and unlocked the door. As he pushed the door open he took the key out of the lock and put it in his pocket.

When they saw all the glass tanks and the trapped water creatures they were horrified. Suddenly Raggie barked "Woof someone is, coming hide!'"

Gordo and Lizzie looked around the room for somewhere to hide. There was some old sacks in one corner so they dashed over to the corner and hid under the sacks just in time. Loki and two goblins came into the room. He checked to make sure that all the tanks were there and no one had escaped. Loki shook the tank which contained the King and Queen frog. "What happened with the water how did the tunnels fill back up?" he growled.

"We don't know" lied the King "the noise of the tunnels flooding woke us up!"

One of the goblins started to laugh "Perhaps those stupid dwarfs broke the dam by accident, if they did they probably drowned and we will have to find more slaves".

Under the sacks Gordo started to move but Lizzie grabbed him and kept him still. Loki was still suspicious.

"Go to the dungeons and check to see if all the land creatures are still there" he growled at the goblins. "If any of them is missing let me know straight away!" Loki turned on his heel and walked out of the room, the goblins followed him.

When the goblins had gone down the corridor and they couldn't hear them any more Gordo, Lizzie and Raggie cautiously lifted the sacks which hid them and looked down the corridor.

"Woof, lets follow them, they might lead us to Chloe" barked Raggie.

As he turned to follow the goblins Fergus shouted "WAIT! You promised to help me free the Duke and Duchess and what about the other aquatic creatures?"

Raggie turned back into the room "Woof, sorry, I got a bit excited about finding Chloe, of course we will help" he barked.

Gordo and Lizzie were already examining the glass tanks. They were trying to figure out the best way of getting the water creatures out without hurting them. They were trying gently tip the tanks to pour the water out with the water creatures but the tanks were too heavy!

"Use your axes" said Fergus.

"We don't want to hurt anyone by accident" said Gordo.

"What if we hit the tanks from either side at the same time?' asked Lizzie.

"That might work said the Duke, try it on our tank first. We don't mind!"

Lizzie and Gordo stood at different ends of the tank and counted to three. Then they both hit the front end of the tank as hard as they could at the same time. There was a loud crack and the front of the tank broke into hundreds of little pieces. The water in the tank flowed out like a big wave carrying the frogs safely into the water. Fergus looked anxiously into the water until he saw them hop out of the water then he jumped for joy. Once they were satisfied that the frogs were OK, Gordo and Lizzie went to the next tank and freed the prisoners. Soon they had broken all the tanks and freed all the prisoners. All the water creatures we very happy to be freed from the tanks.

"We would like to help free the land creatures" said the Duke "but we can't help until those pipes are repaired so we can swim up to the higher levels".

"We will help you fix them, while Raggie finds the dungeons" said Gordo and Lizzie".

The Frogs said they would show Lizzie and Gordo where to find the supplies they needed to fix the pipes.

Raggie put his nose to the ground and started to follow the goblins to the dungeons. "Wait for me" shouted Fergus "I know a shortcut".

Fergus led Raggie trough the tunnels to the dungeons. They were entering the lower levels when they heard Loki and the goblins in the corridor ahead. They hid in the shadows and listened.

"All prisoners are here" said a goblin.

"We counted them twice" said the other.

"Quiet" shouted Loki as he pulled a red communication crystal from his pocket.

"Bring the girl, the dwarfs and the Fairy Godmother to the throne room now!" shouted a voice. The goblins were scared as they recognised Nyx's voice.

"What do we do now? The dwarfs have gone missing since the dam broke" said one of the goblins.

"Don't worry about them! They won't be bothering anyone again" said Loki "Bring me the girl and the Fairy".

Raggie and Fergus watched from the shadows as Chloe and a Fairy were pulled from a cell and dragged along the corridor. Fergus had to stop Raggie leaping after Chloe and the goblins.

"We have to free these creatures first. Then we will have an army to rescue Chloe" said Fergus.

A water sprite was left to guard the prisoners. He looked really sad. Suddenly Fergus hopped out of the shadows towards the guard. The water sprite jumped to his feet and ran across the room. He grabbed Fergus,

Raggie was scared that he would hurt Fergus so he jumped out from the shadows growling.

"Woof, drop the frog! If you hurt him you will be sorry!" barked Raggie. The water sprite jumped back in surprise still holding Fergus.

"It's OK" shouted Fergus "Raggie I would like you to meet my cousin Hydro".

Raggie stopped growling and wagged his tail.

"Woof, pleased to meet you" barked Raggie.

Hydro was surprised to see his favourite cousin and a funny green dog standing in the dungeons.

"What are you doing here? Did you come to help? Have you seen my Mom and Dad? How did you get here?" all the questions came out at once.

"Slow down, slow down" said Fergus laughing.

Raggie explained how they had found the water creatures trapped in another room and how they helped them escape. He told Hydro about Chloe and her Granny the head of the F.B.I. and that she would come to arrest the bad creatures. Unfortunately Hydro's parents were not in the other room. Hydro knew where the goblins kept the spare key and showed it to Raggie. Hydro then helped them rescue the land creatures from the cells.

"It's about time you showed up" shouted Peter hugging Raggie.

"I thought you were never coming" said Daithí as he joined the hug.

"I have never been so glad to see a green dog in my life" said Lir

Hydro showed them a short cut which would lead them all back to where Gordo, Lizzie and the water creatures were working to fix the pipes. Some of the land creatures offered to stand guard in the dungeons in case the goblins came back. There were happy hugs all round as Gordo and Lizzie recognised their friends. Lir wanted to fly out to bring an urgent message to King Blackthorn. Daithaí said he would go with Lir to magically protect him as they swam out the water tunnel. One of the water sprites splash offered to show them the way.

CHAPTER 14 – PALACE OF THE BOGS

Meanwhile Chloe was being dragged upstairs and through corridors by a goblin and Loki. She was frightened and wanted to know what was going on.

"Be quiet child" said Loki "or we will tie you up as well so you can't make any noise!"

Chloe became quiet but did stick her tongue out at Loki and it made her feel much better. Chloe tried to remember all the turns and corridors she saw in case she managed to escape, but it was very difficult as the goblins were running to keep up with Loki. Soon they reached the throne room, the goblins stopped just inside the massive golden doors. Chloe stopped and stared.

The throne room was a living room. Tall trees grew side by side and created the walls with their branches growing together to make a leafy roof. Glow worms lived on the branches and lit the room with a soft yellow glow. There was a river around the edge of the room which had small streams flowing in and out of a beautiful lake which was in the middle of the room.

Water lilies grew in the lake but the beautiful flowers had been burnt and chopped up by the horrible goblins. Beautiful bridges of gold at intervals allowed land creatures to cross to the middle of the room where small floating platforms allowed them to go out onto the lake if they wished. At the other end of the room there was a platform which was surrounded by flowers and vines. To one side of the platform was a golden throne on its side which had been flung there by the goblins when they took over the palace. The other throne was now in the middle of the platform and sitting on that throne was the hooded figure of Nyx.

Nyx was dressed in black with a black cloak pulled up over her hair and she wore a mask which was frightening. Before her, two giants held a pixie who was slumped between them. To either side of the platform there were ugly iron cages the kind used for dangerous animals in the human world. Nyx gestured to Loki and the goblins threw Chloe and the Fairy into one of these cages. Then they turned their attention back to the pixie in the middle of the room. Chloe recognised him as Fionn the Sandman from the picture on the walls of the Sandcastle. Nyx was questioning him and every now and then sparks would shoot out of her fingers towards him. The pixie would scream in pain and then would shout 'NO' at Nyx.

Chloe had sat down in the corner of the cage and started to cry, her hair covered her face. The Fairy turned to Chloe

111

"Are you alright little girl?" Chloe lifted her head to look at the Fairy. As she brushed her hair back from her face, the Fairy gasped

"Oh my Chloe! How did you get here are you OK?"

The Fairy scooped Chloe into her arms and gave her a big hug. Chloe felt strangely happy and safe when the Fairy hugged her

"Do I know you?" asked Chloe curiously.

The Fairy was agitated and flapped her wings in distress she was talking to herself.

"How did this happen? Does Nyx know? What are we going to do?" she whispered to herself.

Chloe coughed and the Fairy turned to her.

"My name is Susie, I am your Fairy Godmother" she said quietly. "We are in quite a pickle" she said sadly.

Chloe was staring at Susie

"I know you! You come to me at night time when I can't sleep and stay with me until I sleep' said Chloe.

Susie was delighted that Chloe knew her. She explained that Nyx had kidnapped her in an effort to get her to use her magic on the Sandman to make him tell her everything so Nyx could get into the Sand mine and access the Sleeping Sand. The reason they picked Susie was because she was one of the most powerful truth Fairies in Fairyland. They knew she looked after a child who lived near a doorway to Fairyland and they were trying to find out who that child was. They hadn't yet figured out if the child was a boy or a girl. Once they knew they could trick the child into Fairyland and then make Susie use her magic to protect the child. Then they could steal Susie's magic and use it to find out how to get into the sand mines. Susie was very upset.

"Now that they have found you, I will have to help them or they will hurt you" Susie sobbed.

Chloe put a comforting hand on Susie's shoulder.

"Calm down" she said quietly "they don't know that you are my Fairy Godmother. Queen Rose and King Blackthorn asked me to come to Fairyland to help find the Sandman. So as long as they don't know who I am, it will be OK."

Chloe explained that she was in search of the two plants for the F.B.I. and was in the wrong place at the wrong time. Loki and his goblins found her and her friends and dragged them in here. She told Susie about Raggie and how he was not captured and that he would bring help from the F.B.I. Susie was glad to hear that Nyx did not know of her link to Chloe and told Chloe that no matter what happened she must not tell them. She had to pretend that Susie was just another Fairy.

Chloe moved to one side of the cage and sat in the corner watching everything that was happening. Susie stood on the other side of the cage her hands gripped the bars as she watched the Sandman, as if she could lend him strength to refuse Nyx the answers she was looking for. Nyx held up her hand "Enough! We are wasting our time with this one. Bring me the Fairy" commanded Nyx. The goblins threw the Sandman into a cage near Chloe and Susie.

Two of the goblins came over to the cage and tried to pull Susie from the cage. Chloe stood up and sidestepped toward the door of the cage. As the goblins struggled to pull Susie from the cage, Chloe slipped out of the cage and started running towards the door into the other part of the palace. Just as she reached the door and began to hope she could get free, the doors slammed shut in her face. She was picked up by invisible hands and turned around in mid-air.

"What do we have here?" asked Nyx. Chloe was dangling over the main pool as Nyx carried her across the room by magic.

"We found her and a pixie and a leprechaun snooping around outside" said Loki.

"She had an F.B.I. homing beacon, we brought them in because we didn't want them to report back to the F.B.I." said Loki.

"My what is the world coming to" mused Nyx "the F.B.I. must be getting soft to allow a human girl to be their agent, no special skills, no magic or anything" laughed NYX.

Suddenly Chloe found herself flying across the room as Nyx flung her back into the cage. Susie looked on in fright and reached for Chloe. Chloe was afraid that Susie might show Nyx that she knew Chloe and then Nyx would use Chloe to get her hands on Susie's magic. Chloe shouted at Susie "Get away from me you horrible Fairy! You are just as bad as her!"

Susie drew back from Chloe with a surprised and hurt look on her face. The goblins slammed the door of the cage shut. Nyx was laughing

"All you Fairy Godmothers have a soft spot for the weak humans" she said to Susie. Nyx started questioning Susie about the child she watched over.

"We know the child is near the doorway" Nyx hissed and she pointed at Susie, sparks shot out of her fingers into Susie and Susie yelled in pain.

"You will never find him" said Susie through clenched teeth.

Nyx started to laugh

"You stupid Fairy, now we know we are looking for a boy".

Susie looked horrified as Nyx laughed some more. Chloe was delighted that Susie had managed to fool Nyx.

"Get a list of all boys living within 10 Fairy miles of the Cherry Tree Station doorway" Nyx ordered Loki. Loki saluted and ran down the corridor. Nyx kept questioning Susie to see if Susie would narrow the search. Chloe was close to tears by the time Nyx had finished. Susie got thrown into a different cage nearer the throne so Chloe wasn't able to see if she was OK. Susie was slumped in the bottom of the cage and was not moving.

Nyx called for food, wine and entertainment to be brought in. Suddenly the room was full of goblins rushing around. They brought in a gold table and placed it on the platform in front of Nyx, then they brought in more food than Chloe had ever seen in her life and put it on the table. Chloe was hungry and her stomach started to growl. Nyx laughed and threw her some bread like she was an animal in a cage. Chloe waited until she had seen Nyx eat some of the same bread before she ate hers. Nyx clapped her hands and more goblins came in. These were dressed in strange clothes which were brightly coloured and had amazing patterns on them. These goblins were the entertainment, they were clowns and they juggled balls and knives. They tripped each other up and each one tried to outdo another. It was mayhem. Nyx was eating her food and clapping her hands.

CHAPTER 15 – ESCAPE

"Psst, over here!" said a strange voice.

Chloe looked around trying to find out where the sound was coming from, but she couldn't see anything. Then a small green frog hopped in through the bars of her cage. "Are you Chloe?" the frog asked. "I am Fergus and Raggie sent me to get you". Chloe was delighted to see a friend and was even happier to know Raggie was OK and that he was organising a rescue.

"Can you please help the Sandman and Susie the Fairy Godmother too?" asked Chloe.

Fergus hopped over to the Sandman's cage and talked quietly for a little while. They both looked towards Susie's cage and shook their heads. It was too close to Nyx for them to rescue her. Fergus cautiously hopped over to Susie's cage to make sure she was OK. He handed her a small key and a small piece of paper. Susie nodded sadly and put her head back on her lap. Fergus hopped back to the Sandman and unlocked his cage then he hopped back to Chloe's cage and unlocked it.

"We have to go now" he whispered. "You need to eat this plant it will help you breathe underwater – we are swimming out through the underwater tunnels because the goblins can't follow us there" said Fergus.

He explained that Susie was too close to Nyx to rescue now but he had given her a key and a map to the underwater passages. Her magic would protect her underwater. She agreed to stay behind until Chloe and the Sandman were safely in the tunnels because she didn't want to ruin their escape attempt. Fergus told Chloe that Peter had transmitted their last coordinates to the F.B.I. and that Lir has gone for help with Daithí. He told her that Gordo and Lizzie had freed the water creatures and the land creatures from the dungeons and that all prisoners except Chloe, Susie and the Sandman were already safe. The water creatures were waiting for the reinforcements and the F.B.I. so they could lead them to the palace to help free the palace and capture Nyx and her followers.

Chloe put the plant in her mouth and chewed, it tasted like strawberries Chloe liked strawberries. Fergus hopped over the lake and slipped into the water without making a ripple. He disappeared under the water for a few moments. Then he popped up to the surface and waved at Chloe and the Sandman. Chloe started to run towards the lake. She was aware that the Sandman was running beside her, she saw the goblins stop what they were doing out of the corner of her eye and they she was beside the lake. She knew how to dive into water because her Dad had showed her how to dive and swim when she was younger. She could see Nyx open her mouth to say something and saw her arm move to point at her and the Sandman. Then Chloe and the Sandman hit the water at the same time. Chloe was holding her breath. A strange creature took her by the arm and continued dragging her down deeper into the water and along a tunnel. Chloe's lungs felt like they were going to burst then she remembered that the plant allowed her to breathe under water and she cautiously took a big breath and was surprised not to swallow water. The creature guided her through the tunnels for what seemed like hours, turning right then left, swimming around corners and through archways. Chloe was completely confused after a few turns.

Soon they swam upwards and exited into an underground room deep within the palace. Here Fergus introduced Chloe to Hydro the water sprite. Hydro had guided her through the maze of tunnels and made sure they didn't get lost. Chloe thanked Hydro and looked around to see the Sandman pop to the surface in the pool. She was glad he was safe but very sad not to see Susie emerge behind him.

"I waited for Susie near the palace pool, but it was surrounded by goblins so there was no way she could have escaped that way" said the Sandman sadly.

Chloe climbed out of the water into the room and started to wring the water from her clothes. As she did this she heard the sound of running feet and "Woof, Woof, Woof" coming from the corridor.

She turned to see a very happy looking green dog run towards her. Raggie was delighted to see her again. He jumped towards her and knocked her back into the water. Chloe was so happy to see him she didn't mind. She gave him a big hug and he licked her face. As she climbed out of the water for a second time Peter, Daithí, Gordo and Lizzie ran into the room. They all hugged Chloe and then the Sandman.

Peter waved his arms and said "tirim" and suddenly Chloe was dry from head to toe and so was Raggie. She laughed and gave Peter a big hug.

"We have to rescue Susie!" said Chloe.

Chloe explained that Susie was her Fairy Godmother and that Nyx wanted to use her to get information out of the Sandman. She was worried that Nyx would hurt her now that both she and the Sandman had escaped. The group sat down and tried to figure out the best way to rescue Susie and trap Nyx and her followers inside the palace. The Duke and Duchess of Frogs hopped into the room closely followed by Jack and some Fairies from the F.B.I. Peter had a strange crystal in his hand which glowed blue, Chloe could hear Granny Pat's voice issuing orders.

Before she could say anything Peter put his finger to his lips and handed her a note. On the outside it read "PLEASE READ ME NOW" Chloe curiously opened the note:

"This note will vanish in 30 seconds please read carefully!

"Chloe darling I am so happy you are safe, Jack will guide you safely back to the rainbow. Before you say anything only your group, Peter and King Blackthorn and Queen Rose know that I am human and that you are my beautiful, brave granddaughter. We fear that some of the Fairies in the F.B.I. are part of Nyx's followers and that they may be giving her information. We do not want her to know of our relationship as you will then be in danger."

As Chloe finished reading the note it turned into a rainbow which shimmered in the air and then vanished. Chloe said nothing to indicate that she knew Granny Pat but instead reported the situation in the throne room to Jack and the other F.B.I. as if she was just another agent. The information was relayed to the headquarters by the crystal and then Chloe could hear orders being issued to the agents and volunteers who had come to rescue the prisoners and capture Nyx.

Jack led them all through the land tunnels to the outside where boats towed by beautiful swans were ready to take them to the rainbow station and safety.

"I want to stay and help" said Chloe and the others agreed.

But Jack shook his head "We have the situation under control. My orders are to get you all to safety. Important people are waiting for you".

Jack led the little group onto one of the boats. This time Hydro, Fergus and the Sandman joined them. Jack gave the swan directions and it started flying across the Bog of Frogs bringing Chloe and her friends with it as it went.

The swan gracefully touched down beside a small island in the middle of a large lake. There was a little cottage on the island that looked deserted and was boarded up. Jack noticed the curious looks from Peter and Daithí.

"This is one of the emergency stations, which are only used in special circumstances" explained Jack. Then he led them around to the back of the cottage and to the back door. It looked very dirty, Jack took a crystal from his pocket and in response several crystals shone creating little rainbows in the air. They were embedded in the door and only shone when the master crystal was close. Jack pressed the master crystal to several of the colourful crystals and then the door swung open.

Chloe peered through the door it looked dark and scary inside and the floor was broken showing a dark cellar underneath. Jack ushered them all inside, Chloe screamed when she found herself pushed towards one of the holes in the floor and then looked on in amazement when Raggie stepped out into mid-air wagging his tail.

"Woof, the floor just looks broken but it is painted that way".

Jack closed the door when everyone was in. They were plunged into darkness for a few seconds and then the ceiling lit up in bright colours which were swirling around and changing patterns. It was beautiful, Chloe looked down at the floor and was amazed when she realised that the floor was indeed painted to look like there were holes showing an old cellar below full of dirty water.

Jack explained that this was a painting completed by the research and development department, they were experimenting on illusions and safe ways of stopping people going into restricted areas by making them think it was impossible to get there. Jack pulled a plate out of the rack on the wall and a trapdoor opened in the floor with a slide that looked familiar. One by one they slid down the slide to the lower level, where a carriage was waiting for them. Inside the carriage there were magic lunchboxes and drinks for everyone in case they were hungry.

Soon the carriage stopped at a large station. The middle of the station looked like the middle of a wagon wheel with rainbow roads leading outwards in all directions. There were no names on any of the tunnels and nothing to show where they went or where they came from. There was another carriage at one of the other platforms. Chloe was looking at it curiously when she noticed the rest of the group had started up the spiral staircase leading to the next level of the station. As she ran across to join the group she saw something small shining dimly on the floor. It was a communication crystal she picked it up and put it into her pocket.

There was only one door leading from the station and it had a large circle on it. Jack walked up to the door and looked into the circle. As he did so beams of light shone out of the hole across his face. A voice said "Authorisation granted", the door opened and they stepped into a small room. Jack pressed a button on the wall and several seconds later the wall disappeared and they found themselves in Granny Pat's office. Chloe ran across the room and gave her Granny a big hug.

Then she noticed that King Blackthorn and Queen Rose were sitting down on the sofa.

She turned around "Sorry, I didn't see you there" she said.

"Not to worry, we are glad to see you safe, as is agent Pat we see" said Queen Rose laughing.

Raggie, Chloe, Peter, Daithí, Fergus and Hydro gave their report in detail to the King, Queen and Granny Pat. They were interrupted by questions occasionally. When they were all finished they were exhausted. Chloe wanted to know what happened when the F.B.I. went into the palace to rescue everyone and capture Nyx.

Granny Pat pressed a button on her remote control and the wall slid to one side showing the giant TV screens. On these screens were live feeds from various F.B.I. agents in the palace. On some of them were replays of the action which happened earlier. "Unfortunately Nyx and Loki escaped with some goblins, they took Susie with them" said Granny Pat sadly.

"We have to rescue her" shouted Chloe is distress.

"We don't know where they went yet" said King Blackthorn gravely.

Chloe started to cry, Queen Rose put her arm around her shoulders and promised that they would not stop searching until they found her. Chloe wanted to help but the Queen said she would have to go back to the human world for a while and that as soon as they had news they would let her know and she could come back and help.

King Blackthorn thanked Hydro and Fergus for their part in freeing the prisoners and awarded them with special titles of 'Defender of Fairyland'. They both received a special crystal from King Blackthorn which would grant them safe passage throughout Fairyland. They could both ask for anything they wanted. Both of them asked for the same thing, help from the King and Queen to rebuild the Bog of Frogs and help to rebuild the homes of the prisoners who were captured by Nyx and her followers. The King readily agreed and asked if they would like anything for themselves. Fergus asked if he could visit Chloe and Raggie in the human world to stay friends, the king smiled and said yes. Hydro asked for a little sister like Chloe, Queen Rose laughed and said they would see what they could do about that.

Peter said that he would take Chloe back home through the Cherry Tree Station and promised to make sure Chloe got there safely. Granny Pat walked them out. On the way out Granny Pat said that Chloe's Mom and Dad didn't know she was head of the F.B.I. as it was a secret and asked her to keep it that way. Chloe promised to keep everything a secret. Before Chloe went into the Little Fish Ponds station she asked where the Sandman was. Granny Pat told her that he was back at the Sandcastle repairing the damage and getting ready for a long night of catching up. It would take a few nights before everything was back to normal but Granny Pat has assigned some trusted F.B.I. agents to the Sandcastle so he would be safe. Chloe was delighted Fionn was back home and working to restore magic and happiness again.

Chloe gave Granny Pat a hug and went into the rainbow station at Little Fish Ponds. This time it was brightly lit and there were Fairies walking around getting onto carriages and arriving from other stations. In the middle of the station were five small ponds surrounding one large pond. Each little pond was full of beautiful goldfish. In the middle of the large pond was a huge statue of a fish and its scales changed colour and shimmered like a rainbow, it was beautiful. Chloe took the slide to Departures and got into the carriage going to the Cherry Tree Station. It was a short and uneventful rainbow ride.

When they got to the Cherry Tree Station Peter led Chloe to the entrance to the human world and carefully looked around to make sure no one was watching and then opened the door to allow Chloe and Raggie back into the human world. Chloe and Raggie said goodbye to Peter and went back out into their garden. As the passed through the door to the garden Raggie's fur changed from green back to normal, he was happy he was his usual golden cover. "Woof, green does not look good on me" barked Raggie. Chloe laughed and scratched him behind the ears.

Chloe's Daddy was bringing the hose around from the back garden to wash his car. Chloe ran over to him and gave him a big hug and Raggie jumped up and licked him on the nose.

"Wow, that was nice" he said "do you want to help me wash the car?" he asked.

"Sure" said Chloe and Raggie barked.

"Excellent" said her Daddy "I will grab a bucket and a sponge for you".

By the time he got back with the bucket and sponge Chloe was fast asleep under the cherry tree and Raggie was curled up beside her in the sun. Chloe's Daddy smiled and left her to sleep while he washed the car.

After a while Chloe's Mom came out with some lemonade and cake for Chloe and her Daddy because they were working so hard.

"I can't believe that Child is asleep again" she said to Chloe's Dad "She has been sitting there all morning reading a book, how can she be so tired?"

Raggie opened one eye and wagged his tail with a big doggy grin on his face. He thought to himself if they only knew how far we travelled today!.

THE END

Lightning Source UK Ltd.
Milton Keynes UK
UKOW04f2350080615

253130UK00001B/26/P